KRAKEN

ERIC S. BROWN

SEVERED PRESS
HOBART TASMANIA

KRAKEN

WWW.SEVEREDPRESS.COM

ISBN: 978-1-925342-99-4

PROLOGUE

Captain Ivan Ivonava smiled as he strolled lazily along the *Pleasure Bound*'s deck. All around him his passengers were enjoying the sun. Husbands and wives lay sprawled in comfortable chairs, soaking up its rays. Here and there, elderly couples were busy playing shuffleboard. A teenager with headphones over her ears stood at the side railing, bopping her head to music so loud, Ivonava could make out a few notes of it as he passed by her.

It was a beautiful day and all was right with the world. His smile grew even wider as he reached the *Pleasure Bound*'s bridge and found yeoman Reeves waiting on him. Reeves handed him a mug of perfectly iced ice. He took it, nodding his gratitude as he moved on to take a seat in his command chair.

Charlton Merrick, his XO, approached him. "Everything is nominal. The lights are green and the decks are clean."

Ivonava chuckled at Merrick's odd expression. It was one the man used ever since he had taken his job aboard the *Pleasure Bound* many years ago.

The *Pleasure Bound* was one of the most luxurious and high-tech cruise liners in the world. Ivonava took great pride in being her captain. He settled in his chair, relaxed, and took a long sip of his tea.

"Sir," Marcus Thacker, the *Pleasure Bound*'s sonar officer, called to him. "I hate to bother you, sir, but…"

Ivonava sighed and shifted in his chair to look towards Thacker at the sonar station. "Don't tell me, let me guess, your phantom is still there?"

Thacker nodded. "It sure is, sir. As you know, it has been with us for the last two days now."

"How could I possibly forget, Mr. Thacker?" Ivonava glared at the sonar tech. "You remind me every chance you get, do you not?"

"Sir, I just…" Thacker started.

"Stop it, Thacker," Ivonava ordered. "I know whatever it is out there worries you, but you yourself have admitted it has to be biologic in nature. It's not pirates or they would have made their move by now, knowing that we would have long ago detected their presence."

Thacker kept his mouth shut but his discontent was clear.

Ivonava waved a hand dismissively. "Let it go, Thacker. I'd wager it's nothing more than an overly friendly group of dolphins."

"But sir…" Thacker started one more time.

"Let it go, Thacker," Ivonava's tone took on a sharp edge that promised retribution. "I don't want to hear any more about our shadow out there under the waves, period. And I can promise you that if I do, you'll find yourself demoted to the janitorial staff until we reach the next port."

Thacker nodded, defeated. "Yes, sir."

"Now, Mr. Merrick," Ivonava turned his attention back to his XO. "What do we have on the agenda for today?"

I

DESRON 22 was composed of four destroyers and an odd-ball group of six frigates. Captain Wirtz stood looking out the bridge window of the USS *Peterson*. He was the second ranking officer of the DESRON. Only Surface Community Captain, Marcus, outranked him. Captain Marcus was aboard the USS *Whiteside*, the DESRON's flag ship. This whole OP was a FUBARed dream of command's and even Marcus wouldn't argue with him on that one. They were far outside of normal SOPs with this exercise but the brass wanted DESRON 22 shook down and combat ready ASAP. This OP was supposed to get both the ships and their crews into proper condition for real deployment. Wirtz knew the ships and crews did need the shakedown but why so far out in the middle of nowhere, he wondered.

The DESRON was for all intents and purposes "off the grid." The region of ocean they were operating in contained nothing of importance and was as far from the Atlantic shipping lanes as it could get. With the rising tension between the Soviets and the US, he could understand the need for secrecy and urgency, but the way he saw things, this shakedown could have run a heck of a lot closer to home. Doing so would have minimized the risk for all involved.

With a shrug, he admitted to himself things could have been worse. At least the weather was nice. The skies were as blue as the water and the long-range forecasts called for more of the same. He passed command of the *Peterson* to his XO, Charles, and left the bridge, deciding to enjoy the sun.

As soon as he hit the deck, he fished a smoke from the pocket of his uniform and lit up. Maybe it wasn't proper protocol, but he needed one and the more senior members of the *Peterson*'s crew were long used to his bad habit.

From where he stood, he could see the USS *Whiteside* ahead of the *Peterson* and in the center of the DESRON's formation. Bringing up the flag ship's other flank was the USS *Arrington* with Captain Holland as its CO. He couldn't see the USS *Emerson* but he knew she was at the loose formation's rear. Her captain, Davis, was like most of the personal in DESRON 22, new to the battlegroup. From what Wirtz had heard of her though, he was impressed. She graduated top of her class, rose through the ranks fast, and after only a year of her own command, already had the rep of being as tough as nails. She was the youngest of the four captains of DESRON 22 but Wirtz reminded himself not to treat her as such. He was an old sailor and often slipped when it came to things like female captains. He equally didn't want to do anything to offend her or worse, damage either of their careers with his lack of understanding when it came to all things the world deemed "politically correct."

Turning his attention back to DESRON 22 itself, he frowned. DESRON 22 was overly heavy in anti-air, guided missile destroyers and lacking in anti-sub firepower. From what little he knew of DESRON 22's post shakedown orders, that lopsidedness would come in handy but for now, if they were engaged, out here, alone, they would be more vulnerable than they should. Both the Soviets and the current day terrorists, who were the primary threats, preferred the use of subs to surface vessels.

Wirtz sucked hard on his cigarette, letting its smoke fill up his lungs. The likelihood of any kind of attack was very small. The Soviets weren't ready to really start the war they were threatening and most terrorist groups knew better than to pick a fight with a United States battle group. Still though, Wirtz couldn't shake the feeling that something bad was waiting for them out here.

****

Lex shivered in the darkness. The sound of water dripping from the dinged piping that ran across the room's ceiling was his only company. It held a steady, slow rhythm and almost seemed to echo off the walls around him. Lex was freezing. Somewhere beyond the room he was barricaded in, the sun was shining and the temps were warm. He imagined a bright sun beaming down on the decks of the *Pleasure Bound.* And that's how things should have been. Mary had talked him into taking this cruise to escape the deadlines and pressure of his work. It cost more than they could really afford but Mary argued that if he didn't get the time off, he would burnout and they would lose everything anyway. Lex gave a cold laugh at the thought. Burning out was always a risk for any entertainer who had to push his or herself not only to find and get work but to produce the work itself.

Three years back, Lex had caught what he thought was the break of his lifetime. A Hollywood studio had picked up the film rights to one of his novels. He had danced around the house, singing happy songs for weeks as he waited on the contract and check to arrive. When they had and he held the check in his hands, all he could do for those first few hours was stare at it. By the standards of most folks, it wasn't like winning the lottery but to a full time writer, it was an answer to his prayers. The check was large enough to ensure he had *time* to sell something else, time to land more deals, and most of all, it represented freedom for Mary who loathed her job as a social worker. The years she had spent helping others had taken a dire toll on her and the check, at least, set her free.

The two of them squirreled it in their joint savings account and used the money to live on. The years it bought them were a paradise, but as the money in the bank grew less and less, fear of not being able to replace it and stay afloat ate at Lex. He took to doing the budget over and over again trying to find ways to stretch the money further but there was just no way. In the end, even after Mary returned to work, they were so behind it wasn't enough to change the oblivion they were headed towards. Lex fought Mary tooth and nail over taking this cruise but that too proved to be a losing battle. They cashed out the bulk of what was left for tickets and set sail for one last romp. He knew Mary hoped it would stir his creativity again and the work would start coming in again. Lex was just beginning to lighten up and enjoy himself when everything went to Hell aboard the *Pleasure Bound.*

Lex didn't know if there was anyone left alive on the massive cruise liner or if he was the last. The meager backpack of food he had been able to grab during his and Mary's wild flight below deck had run out two days ago. Hunger gnawed at him like a claw twisting in his gut. He had never been so hungry in his entire life. There was nothing for it though. The water from the pipes was all he had to drink. It tasted of metal but it did the job of keeping him alive. Lex wasn't sure what the point of trying to stay alive was. He had no idea if the *Pleasure Bound*'s crew had been able to get off a distress signal or not. The things had come onto the ship so quickly, bringing chaos and death with them.

The chill Lex felt grew colder as he remembered the ship security lady who he and Mary had passed on their way below deck. She had urged them on, moving to stand between them and the approaching monsters. Her shotgun had boomed, spitting death, as he blew one of the monsters apart in the stairwell as they poured down it towards her. Lex had risked slowing enough to glance over his shoulder back at her just in time to see her torn apart before his very eyes. Several of the creatures had dug into her at once and literally ripped her into pieces, blood spraying the walls an explosion of red.

The *Pleasure Bound*'s upper decks and hallways were full of mangled corpses and dismembered limbs. There was blood everywhere—the walls, the floor, even the ceiling. The security lady, though, was the first death Lex had seen happen in front of him and God how he wished it had been the last.

As he and Mary had finally made it into the bowels of the ship, enough to feel safe and start searching for a place to hole up until help came, their assumption that they had left the creatures behind them was proved horribly untrue. One of the things dropped from the ceiling onto Mary. Its arms entwined her as she screamed. Her flesh was pulled away from her bones in chunks as she wrestled with the thing from the depths, trying to break free of its hold. Lex watched her struggle, unable to do anything but shout her name. He had no weapon to fight the creature with and even if he had, the struggle ended in mere seconds with Mary dead and the thing's beak-like mouth made short work of her face, leaving only the white of exposed bone in the places where it made contact.

Lex sobbed in the darkness. Tears streamed down his cheeks and he cursed himself for being so weak. He loved Mary, owed her, but when it came his turn to save her, as she had him so many times throughout their marriage, he had failed her. It didn't matter that the thing that killed her was an abomination that shouldn't exist in the real world; guilt haunted him.

Wiping his eyes with the backsides of his hands, Lex tried to collect himself together. All he really wanted to do was give up and die. With Mary gone, there wasn't much point in living anyway. He knew Mary wouldn't want that, though. She would want him to fight to the end. The cold and dampness of the small storage room he hid in only added to the pain caused by his hunger. Lex's hands gripped the wall as he heaved himself to his feet. His legs were shaky beneath him but he managed to stay on his feet. He had never been an "in shape" sort of guy and the last two days had really taken a heavy toll on him. It was hard to think clearly. Lex knew he had to find a way off the ship. It belonged to the monsters now. He dared not let himself believe they had simply swept through the *Pleasure Bound,* eating their fill of her passengers and crew, only to return to the water. No, somehow he knew there were at least some of the things still onboard, searching for prey that might be left alive like him.

Even if he could get off the cruise liner, that didn't mean he would be safe. The things had come from the water and lived in it. He would need something a heck of a lot faster than a standard lifeboat if he wanted to have half a chance of escaping them. The things were faster in the water than they were out of it and he knew they had scaled the sides of the *Pleasure Bound* like sprinting spiders. Not even the members of the ship's security staff in the deeper areas of the ship, who had some warning that the things were coming, were able to mount a real defense against them, despite having the time to arm themselves. Lex couldn't fight the things. Just one of them was more than a match for him. Running and speed were the only things that might, just might, keep him alive. Finding a means to outrun such monsters though, wasn't going to be easy, if it was even possible.

There had been plenty of time for Lex to sort through the limited contents of the small storage room since he had locked himself inside it. There were plenty of cleaning supplies and nothing else. He wasn't one of the characters he wrote about in his books though, so had no idea had to whip up some makeshift weapon from the chemicals and there was no "Google" from him to research how to either. Lex settled for one of the mops in the closest, breaking off its head so he could use the jagged end of the broken shaft as a spear. It wasn't much, but it was all he had.

Spear in hand, he took a deep breath and opened the storage room's door as quietly as he could. He expected one of the things to be waiting on its other side for him, but there was nothing that he could see outside the door through the crack except the corridor it led into and the eerie, red glow of the ship's emergency lights.

Ever so cautiously, Lex stepped into the corridor, his eyes darting from one end of the corridor to the other and finally back up to sweep over the ceiling. He knew all too well that the things could move across it just as easily as they could the floor. It was "do or die trying" time as

Lex stumbled along the corridor, heading for the stairwell that led up to the *Pleasure Bound*'s upper decks.

****

Commander Derrick Spraker stood on the bridge of the *Peart*. She was one of the six frigates that were a part of DESRON 22. Captain Marcus, the DESRON's CO, had ordered all of the frigates out on recon patrols as part of the shakedown the battle group was running. Spraker was glad to be away from the main body of the DESRON. He ran a pretty loose and laid-back ship. He liked it that way. Captain Marcus was as "by the book" as COs came and the two of them had butted heads several times already since DESRON 22 had formed up. Spraker wished that Captain Wirtz were in overall command. The old guy was pretty laid back too in the areas where it counted. Wirtz was the type of captain you could have an off-duty drink with and shoot the breeze. Spraker knew because they had done just that before. The old guy had some pretty amazing stories to tell. In Wirtz's years in the service, he had seen plenty of action, a lot more than Spraker. Oh, Spraker had lived through an engagement or two during his own time, but nothing like what Wirtz had. He enjoyed the old timer's tales of the navy before everything had become so politically correct and on edge. Spraker couldn't imagine what having a drink with Marcus would be like, but it would surely be anything other than a good time. Marcus had the rule book shoved up his butt so far that regulations vomited out of his mouth in an unending stream. If you thought outside of the box at all, under Marcus's command, you were going to pay for it, regardless of whatever results that kind of thinking brought. You could likely save the entire DESRON with a gutsy move and still find yourself facing court martial.

Spraker grunted and turned to Arron, his first mate. "How you holding up?"

"Bored, sir," Arron grinned.

Spraker chuckled. "Part of the job. You'll get used to it."

"You haven't," Arron reminded him.

"Good point," Spraker admitted. "Let's see what we can do to make things a bit more interesting. Helm, aim west and put the pedal down."

The *Peart*'s bridge crew erupted into laughter as Philips, his helmsman, shouted, "Yes, sir. Westward bound and pedal to the metal."

Spraker felt pride surging inside him at how well his crew functioned, despite the easy atmosphere in which he ran things, as the *Peart* came about smoothly and picked up her speed.

Leaving Arron where he stood, Spraker walked to the joint radar/sonar station where Luke sat. The young man beamed at him as he approached.

"What's out there for us today?" Spraker asked.

"Running a full sweep now, sir," Luke answered, diving into his work.

Luke's happy expression quickly turned into one of utter confusion.

"What?" Spraker prompted him.

"Sir," Luke said, his face turning beet red. "I have a surface contact, two miles out."

"One of the other frigates from DESRON 22?" Spraker asked, hiding his own unease and knowing that no one else was supposed to be anywhere near the location where the DESRON was operating.

"Maybe Commander Cordova has decided to take a little joy ride of his own?" Arron suggested with a wry grin. Cordova was a maverick like Spraker too, albeit a much less competent and controlled one.

"I don't think so, sir," Luke said nervously. "Whatever is out there is huge."

"Military?" Spraker asked, leaning over Luke to look at the screen for himself.

"Negative, sir. She seems to be civilian in nature. Her AIS pegs her as the *Pleasure Bound.*"

"The Pleasure Bound?" Spraker read the name aloud himself.

"What the devil?" Arron blurted, scurrying over to join Spraker and Luke at the radar/sonar station. "That doesn't make any sense."

"Tell me about it," Spraker sighed. It wouldn't be the first time a cruise ship had wandered into somewhere it wasn't supposed to be, but Spraker had a bad feeling that something more was going on in this case.

"Get me that ship's captain on the line pronto," Spraker ordered his comm. officer.

"This is the United States frigate, *Peart.* These waters are off-limits to civilian vessels at this time. Please confirm your identification and we will render any assistance you may need," the comm. officer, Megan, broadcasted over the open channel. After a few seconds ticked by, she repeated the message before finally turning back to Spraker.

"The *Pleasure Bound* isn't responding, sir," the comm. officer said, frowning.

Spraker raised an eyebrow at Arron.

"She's dead in the water too, sir, and looks to be drifting," Luke told them. "Whatever is going on with her is likely a lot more than just a comm. issue."

"Should we check her out?" Arron asked.

"I would love to," Spraker sighed, "but Captain Marcus would have our heads. Let's call it in and see what his highness advises."

Spraker nodded at Megan. "Get me the *Whiteside.*"

"You're on, sir," Megan nodded back at him.

"This is the *Peart.* We've stumbled onto a large, civilian vessel adrift at the edge of the exercise parameter. She's not responding to hails. Please advise."

****

Lex staggered along the corridor. The *Pleasure Bound*'s red, emergency lights cast strange shadows along the walls and over the doorways of the cabins lining the corridor's sides. He was surprised the ship's backup power was still functioning. His whole body ached with sheer exhaustion. In the last three days, he had gotten little more than a few hours of sleep. Partly because every time he closed his eyes, the nightmares came and partly because he was too afraid of what might find him while he slept. He had to stay alert, be ready, in case they did find him. Not that he could fight them. If they found him, he was as dead as the rest of the *Pleasure Bound*'s passengers and crew.

The air stank of rotting flesh, stale blood, and stagnate water. Lex had ripped a piece of cloth from the bottom of his T-shirt and wrapped it over his mouth and nose but it didn't really help. The smells were terrible and ever present as he continued his trek towards the upper decks. Every so often, he would come upon a body and be forced to either step over it or slide passed it by pressing himself against the corridor wall if there was room to do so. More often though, he saw pieces of his once fellow passengers; a mangled hand here, a discarded foot there. The worst he had come across so far was an unidentifiable chunk of meat that was clearly human floating in a puddle of red tinted water just inside one of the cabin doors he passed.

Lex clutched his makeshift spear in a white knuckled grip as a fresh wave of nausea rolled over him. The corridor seemed to swirl around him. He paused, fighting it back, until he could move again without the risk of being doubled over by dry heaves. There was nothing in his stomach to come up but he had to keep reminding his body of that. He knew he was sick, sicker than just from the sights and smells around him. The water Lex had been living on during his time in the storage room was likely contaminated from something.

Something moved behind him. Lex whirled around but whatever had been there was gone. Whether it had rounded the bend in the corridor or disappeared into one of the open cabins, he didn't have a clue and didn't care. His heart pounded in his chest. A sickly sheen of sweat coated his skin. His haggard eyes swept over the corridor, desperately searching for whatever had made the noise he had heard. He raised his makeshift spear, trying to seem larger and tougher than he was. He had read somewhere that if you came face to face with a predator, you should try to convince it you weren't worth the fight it would take for it to have you as its next meal. His nerve broke almost instantly. *Yeah, that's crap,* he thought and turned, breaking into a full-out run. His feet slipped out from under him on the wet metal floor and he crashed downward onto it with a loud grunt. Lex's breath was knocked from his lungs. Even as he gasped for air, he threw himself to his feet, and started to take off running again but a voice stopped him.

"Stop right there or so help me God, I will shoot you," a woman aiming a .38 at his face shouted at him.

"Whoa," Lex blurted out, jerking his hands above his head and letting go of his makeshift spear. It clattered to a rest next to his feet. "I'm human!"

"Really?" the woman snapped at him. "I never would have guessed."

She was younger than he was. Lex guessed she was in her early twenties. Dirty and matted red hair clung to her forehead and her shoulders. Her eyes were green and filled with a mixture of fear and anger. She looked like the kind of person who worked out. Her body was lean and hard. She carried herself with a confident posture that left no question that she meant business. Even so, Lex could see the last three days had taken a toll on her too. Aside from the filth covering her, the woman's eyes were sunken in and her skin was an unhealthily pale.

"Wait," Lex pleaded. "I'm a survivor just like you."

The woman kept her gun trained on him but said, "I'm not going to shoot you unless you give me a reason, okay? The last guy I found alive tried to rape me in my sleep so cut me some slack."

Lex's eyes bugged at what she had just said. "I am so sorry," he offered.

"Shut up," the woman ordered. "We've all been through hell on this ship. What's your name?"

"Lex… Lex Iver."

"From the looks of you, you were a passenger like me," the woman gestured at his ragged clothes.

Lex nodded. "My wife and I…" His voice went out on him as fresh tears stung his eyes.

"I get it," the woman said, filling the unexpected silence. "I'm Trish. You can put your hands down now, Lex. You look like an idiot."

Lex lowered his hands but didn't move to retrieve his spear.

"It's good to meet you, Trish," Lex said, finding his voice again and trying to muster up a smile. "I thought I was the only person left."

"So did I," Trish admitted. "It's a big ship though. There have to be others."

"Like the man…" Lex started and then stopped.

"You and him are the only two I have seen so far," Trish said, glancing around the corridor before she looked back at him. "We can't stay here. We're too out in the open."

"Those things are still aboard then?" Lex asked.

"Some," Trish answered, trying the door of the cabin next to where she stood. It wasn't locked and slid open easily. She gestured for Lex to go on in ahead of her. Once he had, she followed him in and slid the door closed behind them. The room was empty other than its bunk and several cases of half unpacked luggage.

Trish dug in one of the pockets of the jacket she wore and tossed Lex a small, half empty bottle of water. She kept her gun in his sight but at least it wasn't aimed at him anymore.

Lex caught the water, unscrewing its lid, and downed it in one gulp. The water was warm but it tasted like heaven compared to what he had been drinking in the storage room. He stared at Trish, trying to figure her out. She was being rather trusting for a woman who claimed to have recently fought off being raped. He supposed she was as desperate for help and the company of other people as he was.

"How did you survive?" Trish asked, taking a seat on the room's bed.

"I've been hiding in a storage room, down below. It's taken me this long to work up the nerve to try to get off this ship. You?"

"I've been moving around the ship, bouncing from cabin to cabin sort of, hunting for others left alive and food."

"I miss food," Lex said before he could stop himself.

"How long since you last ate something?" Trish asked.

"Since before those things showed up."

"That explains why you look like crap warmed over," Trish laughed.

"You don't look so hot yourself," Lex pointed out with a wry grin.

The moment was what they both needed. For a brief second, there were no monsters, pain, or hunger, only two human beings connecting.

Trish dug in a different pocket and shoved a smashed up pack of crackers at him. What was left of the crackers in the pack was little more than crumps but Lex took it, shaking them into his mouth.

"Best crackers I've ever had," he licked at his lips.

"You got a plan?" Trish asked.

Lex shrugged. "Not really. I figured I would work my way up to the main deck and find one of the motorized lifeboats. Maybe make a run for it."

Trish frowned.

"You got a better idea?" Lex asked.

"No, I don't," Trish answered, "but yours sucks. Even if you found one of the motorized lifeboats and managed to get it into the water, the sound of its engine would draw those things on you like zombies swarming a car."

Lex's shoulders slumped. "You're right. I figured I could outrun them though."

"That's a big gamble to take. I know you have to have seen how fast those things are and they're even faster in the water."

"What other choice do we have?" Lex argued.

"Like I said before, this is a big ship. We keep hiding and wait for help to come. That's the safer thing to do."

Lex shook his head. "It's a big ocean out there too. We don't even know if the crew managed to get out a distress call. This ship has to have drifted off course by now. I mean, only God knows where we are. How can you be so sure anyone will ever find us?"

"Faith," Trish flipped open the chamber of his .38 and counted the rounds in it. "Faith and hope. I've got four rounds left in this thing and there are two of us now. Maybe we should make sure a distress call gets sent out."

"And how do we do that?"

"The backup power is still on," Trish pointed out. "All we have to do is make it to the bridge."

Lex grunted. "Okay. Sounds like a plan to me. I'm in."

Trish smiled at him. "I figured you would be."

Patting the bed, she added, "But first, we both need some rest. You look like you need it even more than I do."

Trish got up and moved aside gesturing for Lex to lie down. "I'll take first watch. You got four hours. Make 'em count."

Lex didn't argue. He hit the bed like a falling rock and stretched out. The last thing he saw before his eyes closed and sleep took him was Trish taking a seat on the floor in front of the cabin's door with her pistol ready in her hand.

****

Lex dreamed of Mary. The two of them lay on the *Pleasure Bound*'s sun deck. He held the latest Harrington novel in his hands but not even its epic space battles could hold his attention. His eyes kept leaving the words on its page to roam over Mary where she was sprawled out in the new two piece bathing suit she had picked up just for their trip together. Her skin was tan and he knew from experience just as soft as it looked. She was so beautiful. How a geek like him had ever gotten so lucky in finding a woman like her, he would never know.

Dark sunglasses covered Mary's eyes and her head bobbed in time to whatever music she was listening to through the earbuds of her MP3 player. Knowing her, it was some Seattle band. When the two of them had met and she had taken him to her apartment for the first time, there was a small, almost shrine to Eddie Vedder. As their relationship went on, that wasn't the only thing that surprised him about her. She seemed the epitome of normal and boring by most folks' standards in public but underneath all that was a woman who loved the grunge scene, practiced survival skills, and bordered on being a full out "prepper." The only celebrity she was more a fan of than Vedder was Robert Downey Jr. Mary swore he was God's gift to woman. That didn't bother Lex, though. In some ways, he was like Downey. He was quirky, smart, and cute according to Mary and she loved him. And when she said those three words, "I love you", to him, Lex more than knew they were true, he felt them in his soul.

The sun was at its zenith in the blue sky above them. There were plenty of other people on the sundeck with them but to Lex, there was only Mary and himself. This was as pretty close to paradise. No work, no deadlines, no bills to worry over, just the best view in the world as Mary rolled over to lay on her stomach, and a good book in his hands.

Like all good things in the world of man though, it was too good to last. The sun was eclipsed by blackness as storm clouds came thundering in out of nowhere. The rain fell suddenly in waves so hard the drops felt like small stones pounding on his skin. Only it wasn't rain. It was water from the ocean spraying upwards over the edge of the deck. Mary was screaming, her beautiful features twisted by fear as she pointed at something behind where Lex sat. Lex started to turn but out of the corner of his eye he saw some *thing* grabbing ahold of Mary. Its arms wrapped about her body. Her skin tore and bled as its tentacles snaked over her naked flesh. Her screams of fear became shrieks of pain.

Lex threw his novel aside, leaping to his feet, to run to Mary as she wailed his name. He never made it to her. The deck in front of him exploded, sending splinters flying to imbed themselves in his legs and the arms he desperately flung in front of his chest to ward them off. The next thing he knew he was on the deck and rolling in the opposite direction he had been running. He caught only a glimpse of the monstrous thing that rose through the shattered deck and writhed about in the air over him before he woke up.

Something smashed into Lex's forehead knocking him backwards. He flopped over onto the bed once more and felt blood trickling from the area just below his hairline into his eyes. Lex shook his head, trying to clear it as the world around him came into focus. Trish stood over him, her pistol in her hand. He saw his blood on the butt of the pistol and pieced together that Trish had just bashed him with it.

"Stop it!" she whispered violently at him. "Don't make me hit you again!"

Lex realized he had been dreaming and must have woken up screaming. Trish had nearly bashed in his skull trying to get him to shut up.

"It's okay," he assured her, rubbing at his aching head. "It was just a nightmare."

Trish looked to relax a bit. "Sorry about your head," she offered.

Lex sat up, swinging his feet off the bed and onto the floor. "You did what you had to do."

Trish changed the subject. "My watch was just about up anyways. I was going to wake you up in a few more minutes."

"I wish you had done it early," Lex commented. "I don't suppose you have any painkillers in that jacket of yours, do you?"

"Fresh out," Trish told him.

Lex frowned. "Your turn I suppose."

"Forget it," Trish offered him a hand up off the bed. "We've been here too long already even without that outburst of yours. We need to get moving."

"To the bridge?"

"To anywhere but here for now," Trish said, already heading for the cabin's door. "We'll figure out the rest as we go."

****

Trish led them through the corridors of *Pleasure Bound.* Lex was more than content to let her do so. It meant she trusted him enough now to let him be behind her; plus, she was the one with the gun. If one of those things came at them, she would have a lot better chance of stopping it than he would with his spear made from a mop handle. Lex had picked up the spear from outside the cabin where they had holed up for his nap. The sleep had done him a lot of good. His mind was clearer than it had been in days. He was sure the clean water and crushed crackers Trish gave him had helped too. His stomach still clawed at him with pangs of hunger, but somehow they didn't seem as sharp or important anymore. The two of them had a shared goal and it gave him purpose. He was beginning to allow himself to hope they really could reach the ship's bridge and get out a call for help. Of course, that meant they would still need to stay alive until that help could reach them but hey, they had made it this far.

They came to stop at the base of the stairwell leading up to the main deck where the bridge was located. There was no sign of the creatures they shared the ship with. Lex used the pause to ask a question that had been bugging him.

"Trish, I've been meaning to ask, how did you get that gun?"

Trish looked at him as if he were crazy. "Did I hit you too hard a while ago or something?" she snapped at him. "We're almost to the bridge and you're worried about where I got this?" She waved her pistol at him.

"I'm fine, thanks," Lex told her trying not to sound bitter about the hard knot of his forehead. "But yeah, I want to know. If I had one when those things came, maybe I could have…"

"Don't go down that road, Lex," Trish warned him. "Your wife is dead. All the ifs, ands, and maybes in the world aren't going to bring her back."

"Still…"

Trish sighed. "I got it from one of the ship's security staff, okay?"

"They just gave it to you?"

Trish shook her head. Lex could see this was an uncomfortable topic for her but he couldn't let it go.

"It was *his*. The guy who tried to rape me."

"Geez…" Lex said, utterly surprised. "You killed that bastard with his own gun? Somehow that seems kind of fitting."

"I guess so, yeah," Trish kept her face turned away from him as she spoke. "He saved me first you know? If it hadn't been for him, I'd be dead now. When those things were pouring onto the ship and rampaging everywhere, he got me out of the worst of it. Took us below deck like what you tried to do with your wife. We locked ourselves in his quarters. I figured we were planning to just wait things out. Apparently, he had other things on his mind."

"And paid the price for them too," Lex added.

"Enough with it, though," Trish said. "We've got more important things to be focusing on than the past."

Lex found he couldn't argue with that and they started up the stair together. Trish stayed in the lead but he followed her closely while keeping an eye out for anything slipping up behind them.

They reached the bridge without incident, but what they found there was nightmarish. The main bridge window had been shattered and looked to have exploded inward from the outside as if something massive has had pushed its way through it. The walls around the window were damaged and bent despite being metal. Lex didn't have a clue what could have done such a thing and wasn't sure he ever wanted to know what was responsible for the damage. The rest of the bridge was in no better shape. Pieces of the ceiling itself and exposed wiring hung downward, dangling into the knee-high water that filled the bridge. It almost looked like a giant wave of some kind had come crashing inside the ship through the shattered window. The smell of rotting meat was more concentrated on the bridge and it was easy to see why. Here and there, bodies floated in the water. Their flesh was gray and puckered. He and Trish did their best to stay clear of them as they started to enter the bridge.

"Wait!" Trish called out to him as Lex was about to step into the water. "Those things might be under the water in here."

Lex recoiled from the bridge's entrance in utter terror, nearly losing his footing on the small set down edge into it. She was right. Those things lived in the water. If they were on the bridge, lying on the floor, waiting, the two of them would never know it until it was too late. He could see from looking at Trish that she had never expected to find the bridge like this. Who would? Sure, there were numerous spots on the ship where water had gotten onboard or been carried aboard by the creatures but still…

"I can see what has to be the radio station from here," Lex said, attempting to sound determined and brave despite the circumstances.

"Great," Trish snorted. "Why don't you grow some wings and just fly over to it?"

"There's no need for that," Lex said. "We're both scared and stressed out but we're still a team, aren't we?"

"Sorry." Trish had jerked up her .38 at the sight of the water and she kept it aim at the stagnate pool that was the bridge's floor. "You're right, okay? I was out of line."

Lex waved off her apology. "What are we going to do?"

"What can we do but try for it anyway?" Trish asked.

"You volunteering?" he asked.

"No. I was hoping you would since I am the one with the gun," Trish said, smirking.

Lex shot her a not-so-happy glare and then stepped into the water before she could say anything else. It was cold. A shiver ran up his spine but he ignored it, plunging further into the water. He splashed across the bridge as quickly as he could, heading for the radio station. He didn't breath again until his hands were clutching his sides then he looked back at Trish.

"Okay. I'm here. Any idea how to work this thing?"

"Pick up the mic-looking thing and start talking into it I am guessing."

"Not helpful," Lex muttered too quietly for her to hear, he hoped.

He picked up the mic and started broadcasting. "Mayday. Mayday. We've been attacked and need help!"

"Tell them who you are you idiot!" Trish shouted at him.

Lex gave her the finger and started again. "This is the cruise liner *Pleasure Bound.* We've been attacked and need help."

Both he and Trish reeled in disbelief as a voice responded to his call.

"This is the *Peart*. We read you *Pleasure Bound* and are already in route to your position. Do not attempt to power up your engines and alter course."

"Thank God," Lex heard Trish sigh.

"I don't think that would even be possible," Lex said over the radio. "This ship is toast."

"*Pleasure Bound*, could you repeat please? Did you say you were attacked?"

"Yes! We've been attacked. Almost everyone on this ship is dead!" Lex answered.

"Who attacked you, *Pleasure Bound?* Pirates? Do you have terrorists aboard you?"

"You wouldn't believe me if I told you." Lex dodged the question knowing no one would ever believe what had happened without seeing it for themselves. He knew too though that he needed to tell the *Peart* about the creatures before she and her crew arrived.

"Just hang in there, *Pleasure Bound*. We're on our way," the voice assured them.

"They sound like they're navy!" Lex smiled. "We're saved! We're really saved!"

Neither he nor Trish saw the creature streaking towards where Trish stood at the bridge's door until it was too late to do anything but scream. The thing reached Trish before she even saw it coming. One of its tentacles lashed outwards from the water, ensnaring the wrist of her gun hand. She cried out in pain as the tiny hooks that lined the tentacle's underside dug into her flesh and sent her pistol flying. It splashed into the water and sunk from sight. Two more tentacles snapped up from the water, closing about her legs. Lex threw himself forward, pushing his body to its limit in an attempt to reach Trish before the thing pulled her under. She was fighting hard against the thing in spite of the sheer shock she had to be feeling. Trish managed to wrench her hands around and grab onto the doorway. She and the thing wrestled in a contest of strength just long enough for Lex to close the distance to them. With a rage-filled cry, he raised his makeshift spear over his head and brought it down into the backside of the creature's body. The creature gave something resembling a squeal of pain and writhed about on the piece of wooden mop that impaled it. Another of its tentacles shot out backwards towards Lex, whipping past his head as he tried to jerk out of its path. It struck so close he could feel the air from the blow on his cheek.

The voice on the radio cried out, asking what was wrong, demanding to know what was happening. Lex had no means of answering it. There was so much more he needed to tell the ship that claimed to be in route. He hadn't managed to tell them about the creatures at all. He hoped they wouldn't arrive just to die like everyone aboard the *Pleasure Bound* had. If they were really navy, they would be armed. Lex hoped they would prove more of a challenge for the creatures and maybe even kick their butts…not that the things had actual butts.

Black blood squirted from around where his makeshift speared pierced the thing's body. It covered his hands. It wasn't warm like human blood and had a slime-ish feel to it. Lex knew he couldn't hold the thing with his makeshift spear so he let go of the weapon. The creature, apparently more injured than he dared hope, streaked away towards the other side of the bridge the second he let go. By the grace of

God, he saw Trish's pistol lying beneath the water on the floor in front of him. His hand broke the water's surface as he snatched it up.

"Run!" he yelled at Trish, charging straight at her. She was too freaked out to hear him or move from his path. Lex plowed into her, knocking her backwards through the bridge's door into the corridor beyond.

He could hear the thing on the bridge moving about in the water and circling around to come at them again. Jerking Trish halfway to her feet, he dragged her along as he ran like hell. Trish righted herself quickly and kept pace with him as they fled. Lex knew there was no outrunning that thing if it really wanted to catch them. He spotted an open door up ahead and pressed onward for it.

Grabbing Trish and hurling through the open door in front of them, he dove in after her and slammed it shut. A quick glance told him that they must be in the captain's office. There was a desk with two chairs in front in the room across from them. An open laptop sat on the desk's top, turned on its side, and there was scattered paperwork and folders everywhere.

Lex whirled around to make sure the door was locked. It was made of metal so he hoped it would keep the monster out at least for a while.

Trish had collapsed against the room's wall. She sat shaking and looking up at him with terrified eyes. "I… I thought I was dead," she told him.

"Me too," Lex agreed. "You're one lucky lady."

The door was solid so there was no way to see if the creature had decided to come after them or not. Lex pressed his ear against the door and listened. If it was out there, it was sure being quiet.

"Glad you got the gun," Trish whimpered.

"How bad did it get you?" Lex asked, reluctantly moving away from the door to check on Trish. He could see red seeping through the cloth of her jeans. Her wrist was a shredded mess of torn and ripped flesh. She clutched it against her breasts as she continued to sob.

"You're tougher than this, Trish," Lex barked at her. "You're a hell of a lot tougher than me anyway. Let me see that wrist. We need to try to do something for it."

"It's bad," she said, sounding as if she was calming down despite her tortured expression of pain. "Check the desk's drawer. Most cabins on TV and in the movies keep a bottle of something strong tucked away there."

Lex did as she told him and sure enough, she was right. There was a bottle of Vodka in the drawer. He rushed over to her side again. "This is going to sting some," he warned her.

"Stop being a baby and just do it," she ordered him, sounding more like the woman he had come to know in the last few hours.

He opened the bottle and poured a good portion of the bottle over her wrist. Trish gritted her teeth and her feet kicked out across the floor as her body shook but she didn't scream. With her good hand, she ripped a piece of cloth from her shirt, taking the Vodka from Lex to pour it onto the cloth before she started wrapping it around her wound.

"You know we're going to have to treat your legs too," Lex said. "God only knows what kind of diseases those things carry."

Trish unbuttoned her pants and slid them over her hips. Lex felt a pang of guilt at the feelings stirred in him by the sight of her flesh before she got her pants down far enough for him to see the wounds on her lower thighs.

"How bad are they?" Trish asked, leaning against the wall, too tired to look for herself.

"They're nothing compared to that wrist. You're going to be fine."

"Good," Trish said, "Because I think I need to pass out now."

****

Commander Spraker felt like bashing in Captain Marcus' head but he tried not to take it out on his crew as the *Peart* poured on the speed towards the civilian vessel, the *Pleasure Bound*. Marcus grated on Spraker's nerves to the point of leaving them raw. It had been like pulling teeth to get permission to leave the established patrol course Marcus had assigned the *Peart*. Marcus had wanted him to simply order the *Pleasure Bound* away from the area where DESRON 22 was conducting its shakedown maneuvers. If Luke hadn't finally made contact with the cruise liner, Spraker might have still been arguing with Marcus over how to handle the situation. There weren't supposed to be any other vessels in this region and the *Pleasure Bound*'s sudden appearance had caught them all off guard.

Luke had made contact with the cruise liner though. She was adrift and whoever Luke had spoken with briefly claimed the ship had been attacked. Luke reported that the man he spoke with seemed to have no radio training or understanding of the protocols for talking over the air. He also reported the man had failed to identify himself. That combined with the man's claims that the cruise liner had been attacked and that most of the people onboard it were dead put Spraker on edge. It just didn't make any sense. Who attacked a cruise liner? Pirates were the most likely explanation but the cruise liner, according to the data Luke had managed to pull up on it, was in the one hundred and fifty thousand ton range. Her passenger capacity was in excess of thirty-six hundred and her crew was listed at a minimum twelve hundred and fifty members. That meant there were at least forty-eight hundred and fifty souls aboard it. No sane group of pirates would ever attack something as large as her in international waters. The risks and costs of taking such a ship just didn't justify such an attack unless there was something special about the *Pleasure Bound* that Spraker wasn't aware of.

Terrorists didn't make much sense either. ISIS and their ilk tended not to target ships. Why strike a target so far away from the population you wanted to instill fear in? Terrorists would have boarded the ship when she left port though and worked from within it but even so, the *Pleasure Bound* was just so large a target. There was a lot easier prey than her out there on the waves to be had. She was a top of the line ship and her security force was not only armed but armed to the teeth by civilian standards. The blueprints of the ship that Luke had pulled up included two well-stocked armories. The manifests of those armories were impressive as they were on paper, but Spraker knew there would be some extra items the cruise line's owner or owners had packed in them as precautions that they weren't going to list on the sort of legal stuff Luke had pulled up.

As thus, Spraker and his crew were going into this blind with no idea of what was waiting on them. The *Peart* was a much smaller vessel at only four thousand tons but her engines were military grade and the *Pleasure Bound* had no chance of out running her. Not that Spraker thought anyone onboard the cruise ship would be dumb enough to try. Plus, being a civilian vessel, the *Pleasure Bound* had no ship-to-ship weaponry. The *Peart* could hold back and blow her out of the water if it came to it. Wouldn't that just look lovely on the six o'clock news? US Naval frigate sinks civilian cruise liner in the middle of the Atlantic, film at eleven.

Spraker frowned. There was just so much he didn't know that he needed to as he sat in his command chair watching Philips at the *Peart*'s helm. They would be coming into visual range with the *Pleasure Bound* any minute now.

Snapping his fingers at Arron, Spraker got his attention. "Prepare boarding parties," he ordered. "Make sure the squad leaders know the folks aboard that ship are civilians and need to be treated as such."

"Yes, sir," Arron nodded and left the *Peart*'s bridge.

"And Arron," Spraker called after him. "Make sure our guys are in full battle gear too. I've got a bad feeling about this one."

Spraker turned his attention back to the view of the waves through the *Peart*'s forward window. He couldn't see enough for his liking so he left his command chair and walked closer to the window. The *Pleasure Bound* was out there waiting on them. He could see her huge form growing closer in the distance.

"Binoculars," he ordered and stuck out his hand. One of his crewmen plopped a pair onto Spraker's open palm. Spraker raised them to his eyes and zoomed in on the *Pleasure Bound*. From how she was moving in the water, it was easy to see she was adrift just as he had expected and the man they had spoken with over the comm. claimed. There were odd blotches of red on the sides of her hull. She was still too far away for

Spraker to make out what the red spots were but they appeared to be moving.

"What in the devil?" he muttered.

"Sir!" the *Peart*'s radar/sonar tech yelled at him. "I have multiple surface contacts all around the *Pleasure Bound!*"

"What?" Spraker snapped at the young crewman. "What kind of contacts?"

"I... I don't know, sir. They're small whatever they are. Not much larger than man-sized."

Spraker knew the *Peart*'s radar and sonar had just undergone massive upgrades but...

"Could they be bodies?" Spraker asked and the bridge went silent around him.

"Maybe, sir," the radar/sonar tech answered. "But if so, they're moving and moving faster than anything human could."

Spraker had heard of schools of dolphin and other sea creatures gathering around ships like the *Pleasure Bound,* especially derelict ones, but surely the *Pleasure Bound* couldn't have been drifting that long could she?

"Philips, kill the engines and bring us to a full stop. We need to know more about what's going on over there before we just go plowing into the middle of it," Spraker barked.

"Yes, sir," Philips answered as his fingers danced over the controls in front of him at the helm.

"Any further word from the *Pleasure Bound?*" Spraker asked Luke.

"No, sir." Megan squirmed in her seat at the comm. console. She and Luke had been working together from the start of all this madness trying to piece together what was happening over there aboard the cruise liner. Luke had even been the one to speak with the man aboard the ship when contact had been briefly achieved. "But Luke said it sounded like the man we made contact with came under attack himself and had to leave the *Pleasure Bound*'s bridge area. I overheard the end of it myself. It really sounded as if the man was fighting for his life," Megan reminded him.

"Blast it!" Spraker raged.

"Should I have Arron hold off on sending over the boarding parties?" Luke asked.

"No," Spraker shook his head. "The sooner we get boots on deck over there, the sooner we'll know what we're dealing with."

"Arron reports the marines are ready to go," Luke informed him while Spraker wrung his hands together.

"Send them in," Spraker told him and raised his binoculars again. Within a mere few minutes, a group of small boats bounced across the waves from the position *the Peart* had stopped at towards the *Pleasure Bound*. Spraker watched them for a moment before returning his gaze to the *Pleasure Bound* herself. The red spots on her hull began to drop into the water, one by one. *What the Hell?* he wondered. It was as if whatever the red spots were sensed or saw the boats approaching the *Pleasure Bound* and wanted to be in the water, out of sight, before they arrived. Part of Spraker wanted to order his marines back to the *Peart,* but there were people over there on that liner that needed help and he couldn't.

****

Lieutenant Page was the CO of the squad in the lead boat heading for the *Pleasure Bound.* Greg sat at the boat's rear, steering it. Clark sat next to Page while Diana sat in the boat's bow, her eyes trained on the large vessel that kept growing larger as they drew closer to it.

"Any idea what those things that dropped into the water were Diana?" Page shouted over the roar of the boat's motor.

"No, sir," Diana shook her head. "Couldn't get a good enough look at them, sir."

Page frowned at her.

"You're not living up to your nickname, Eagle Eyes," he chided her.

"Whatever they were, they weren't human. I can tell you that much," Diana said. "They took off like torpedoes when they hit the water, sir. I don't see any of them around now."

"Maybe they saw us coming and left," Clark said, grinning.

"I wouldn't count on it," Page slapped Clark on the shoulder then turned to Greg. "Bring us in close. We need to get up on deck as fast as we can."

Greg steered the small boat to come up next to the *Pleasure Bound*'s portside hull. Diana used their boarding gear to secure the boat there as Clark fired a grapple up to snag the side of the cruise liner's deck above them. He tested the rope and gave the others a thumbs up sign.

"After you, sir," Clark said, handing the rope to Page. Page glared at Clark but didn't pull rank on him. He just started climbing.

Page, Greg, and Diana were on the deck of the *Pleasure Bound* in record time leaving Clark to stay with their boat below. Page saw Fox and Snapper with the four marines of their squads were also onboard and already fanning out to form a secure perimeter around the area where they all boarded.

"Hey Page!" Snapper called. "What's the drill on this one? Better be weapons hot, man."

Page was in overall command of the three squads. He didn't answer Snapper though. His eyes were glued to the carnage around them. "Geez..."

Some of the squad members were on their hands and knees vomiting onto the cruise ship's deck. The whole area was drenched in sea water, blood, and there were corpses and scattered, torn apart bodies everywhere.

Even Diana, as tough as she was, looked pale as she asked him, "What happened here, sir?"

"Sort of looks like a big bomb went off while everyone was sunbathing," Greg commented. "I've never seen anything like this."

"How could you?" Diana popped him on the backside of his skull. "This is, what, your second OP?"

"He's right though, Diana, and you know it," Page said. "This crap here is seriously some messed up—"

"Lieutenant!" Fox called, interrupting him. "We got movement, sir!"

"Where?" Page demanded to know, racing to where Fox stood with his M4's safety off and the weapon held ready.

"Everywhere I think, sir," Fox stammered, gesturing towards the growing shadows that stretched over the *Pleasure Bound*'s deck and all the doorways that led into the ship's interior.

Page looked for himself, scanning over his entire line of sight, to see nothing. "Are you sure?"

Fox nodded. "Trust me, sir, I am one hundred percent sure. Whatever I saw, they were fast, sir. I mean really fast."

Page sensed Fox wasn't telling him everything. "And?" he prompted.

"Well, sir, I swear I saw one of whatever those things are go straight up that wall over there and disappear onto the level above us."

Page stared at Fox, but as far he could tell, the NCO was telling the truth. Fox was totally shaken up by whatever had seen and Page knew him well enough to know that didn't happen easily.

"Hold position here," Page ordered. "Keep your eyes on each other *and* a sharp lookout for whatever Fox thinks he saw in case they come back."

Page wiped sweat from his brow with the back of his hand, grunting. "And somebody get me a body count on these poor bastards all over the deck. The commander is going to want to know about them ASAP."

****

Commander Spraker couldn't believe what he was hearing as the boarding parties' report came in. Over four hundred civilians found dead on just the *Pleasure Bound*'s main deck and his men hadn't even moved into the ship proper yet. Worse, Lieutenant Page had informed him that count was likely on the low side as so many of the bodies they had found were really just pieces of bodies. The count could be a lot higher than what the lieutenant was guessing and he wanted to make sure that Spraker knew that.

According to Page, there was no sign of an armed attack on the cruise liner's civilian population despite the carnage. None of the bodies had gunshots wounds or anything else resembling man-made ones. There were no signs or traces of explosives being detonated. All the bodies appeared to have been torn and/or slashed apart. Some of them partially eaten from how Page told things and other smaller pieces looked almost digested down to goo that was smeared on the *Pleasure Bound*'s deck and walls.

Page also reported a rather disturbing amount of ocean water aboard the vessel. There were pools of it everywhere almost as if some kind of giant wave had struck the ship, but there was nothing in the area to have caused such a wave as far as Spraker knew. The weather was clear and there were no indications that the *Pleasure Bound* had been damaged in such a fashion as to cause her to take on water.

The whole mess was driving Spraker mad. There were no answers, only more questions that led to even more questions. He sipped at the cup of coffee he had a crewman bring him earlier and leaned back in his command chair. Protocol demanded he fill in Captain Marcus on what he had found, but a snowball had a better chance of surviving in Hell than there was of him doing so before he had at least some answers.

Spraker glanced at his watch. The boarding parties had been onboard the *Pleasure Bound* for almost an hour now and they hadn't dared to make any attempt to truly enter the ship without his approval. With a frustrated sigh, Spraker knew it was time to give them the go ahead.

****

Lex and Trish saw the *Peart* sitting on the distant horizon through the portside window of the *Pleasure Bound*'s captain's office they were holed up in. She was a beautiful sight, all gleaming metal and deck-mounted weapon arrays. The voice they had heard over the radio really did belong to a navy officer and that ship out there represented their ticket off the floating nightmare they were trapped on.

Trish moaned where she lay against the cabin's wall. Lex hadn't been able to move her to the bed. He was too tired and every time he tried, the pain of her wounds was too intense for Trish to stand. Lex couldn't risk the sound of her screams drawing the creature that might still be in the nearby bridge area to them. He was frightened for her. Lex wasn't a doctor, but it didn't take one to know that she had a fever and it was growing with each passing hour. Only God knew what the thing that attacked her might have passed on to her through the wounds it ripped in her flesh.

Lex left the window and knelt beside Trish, placing his palm on her forehead to check her fever again. He took his hand away quickly as she stirred at his touch. Her tired eyes flickered open and she looked at him with great sadness in them.

"It was a navy ship, Trish," Lex whispered to her. "We're going home."

It looked like she tried to shake her head but failed. Her head lolled to the left as she continued to stare at him. "No," she croaked. "If what you're telling me is true, Lex, you have to go. Leave me here."

"Forget it, Trish," he told her firmly. "I'm not leaving you. We're a team, remember?"

Trish laughed and then her body seized up with pain from the movement. She coughed up a mouthful for blood and half spat it out. Globs of it clung to her lower mouth and chin as she spoke. "You barely know me, Lex. You have a chance to live and your wife would have wanted you to take it."

Lex squeezed one of his hands into a fist so tightly that his nails broke the skin of his palm. "Stop it, Trish. Just stop it. We're leaving here together or not at all."

"You have my pistol don't you?" she asked as another coughing fit shook her.

Lex nodded. "I got it."

"Give it to me," she ordered him.

Lex reluctantly handed it over. Trish took it with her good hand, continuing to cradle the other with the mangled wrist to her chest. She flipped the chamber open and took a look inside it.

"You've got three rounds left, Lex. Make them count. For me, okay?"

"What? There are four rounds in the gun. I haven't fired any," Lex protested, failing to understand what she meant until it was too late. Trish raised the gun to her temple, pushing the tip of the barrel underneath her hair to touch her skin, and pulled the trigger. The noise of the shot was muffled by Trish's skull as the bullet entered it. An explosion of blood, bone fragments, and brain matter splattered onto the wall before Trish. Her body slumped forward, the pistol sliding out of her grasp. It clattered to the floor beside her corpse.

Lex was too stunned to react instantly. It took his brain a second to process that horror that had just unfolded in front of him. When what he had just witnessed fully hit him, he let out an almost inhuman whine of hurt and anger. Emotionally, he wanted to grab up the gun and join Trish wherever her soul had gone. The rational part of him, though, took control. He grabbed up the gun, not to kill himself, but to defend himself with. There was no chance the thing on the bridge hadn't heard the shot echoing in the captain's office. Trish had forced him to leave her and move now or be stuck here with that monster out there tearing at the door until it finally got inside.

Unlocking the door, Lex jerked it open, half expecting to see the thing already outside it, waiting on him. It wasn't though. He did, however, hear it splashing about in the water on the bridge. From the sound of things, it was on its way towards him. Lex started running, his legs pumping under him, down the corridor in the direction that led away from the bridge and the monster on it.

The red lights in the corridor were beginning to flicker and grow dimmer as he ran. He figured the *Pleasure Bound*'s emergency power must finally be failing. He wasn't an engineer, so he didn't know if it was just the batteries giving out or if the monsters were behind it somehow. The things gave the impression of being too dang smart for the animals that they were. That ship out there, the *Peart,* if he remembered its name correctly, surely had sent over people to help whoever they could find on the *Pleasure Bound.* Those folks would be armed too, Lex knew. Cutting the power could be a means of the creatures attempting to even the playing field in the cruise liner's corridors.

Lex heard something splashing behind him. He whirled around long enough to fire a single shot in the direction of the noise, without bothering to find a target and aim, then kept right on running. He heard the shot ping against one of the corridor's metal walls and knew he hadn't hit the monster. Still, he hoped the shot would slow it down. As tough and fast as the creatures were, they were flesh and blood just like he was and could be hurt.

Knowing he had to reach the exterior decks because that's where any party that had come aboard would likely be, Lex spotted a stairwell leading up at the end of the corridor and picked up his speed towards it. His breath came in ragged gasps and his vision blurred as sweat poured from his exhausted body but he pushed himself on.

****

Commander Spraker had given the word. Despite the risks involved, the chance of saving anyone left alive on the massive cruise liner outweighed the safety of his men. Lieutenant Page understood the logic behind the choice. Besides, who wanted to live forever? No one who signed up to be a marine that was for sure.

"Okay, Fox, you and your squad hold here. I want the way clear for us if we have to bug out fast, got it?"

"Yes, sir." Fox smiled.

"Snapper, take your men and head aft. I'll take my squad inside here. It's as good an entry point as any I reckon."

Page had just started forward when the door he had picked burst open in front of him. Diana and Greg opened fire on it out of instinct, born of long hours of training. The man who had come bounding out of it threw himself to the deck just in time to keep from being cut in half by their fire.

"Hold fire! Hold fire!" Page yelled. Diana and Greg jerked the barrels of their rifle skyward.

The man on the deck was yelling too. "I'm human! I'm human!" he shouted over and over again.

"Freeze where you are," Page shouted at him, seeing the .38 pistol the man clutched in his right hand. "And toss that weapon away. Now!"

The man did as he was instructed, sliding the pistol over the deck towards Page and his men. Page picked it up as Snapper's squad kept their weapons trained on the man. Diana and Greg moved in to secure him. They took his arms, holding him firmly, as they helped the man to his feet.

The man stunk as bad as everything else on the ship Page had encountered. Page wagered the man had to be surviving in the bowels of the ship without proper food or water for days. The man was lean and teetered on the edge of collapse even with Diana and Greg supporting him. There was blood, not his own, smeared on the clothes he wore and his hair was matted to his scalp by layers of filth and slime.

"What happened here?" Page demanded.

The man met his eyes as he spoke. "Sir, we have to get off this ship now while we still can. Please!"

"We're not going anywhere just yet," Page told the man. "Not until I get some answers. How many more passengers alive are alive in there?" Page gestured at the doorway the man had burst out of.

"Nobody," the man struggled vainly against Diana and Greg's hold on him with a fresh wave of strength. It wasn't enough for him to break free though, so he stopped. "I'm the only one alive on this ship, sir. Everyone else is dead."

"Son," Page said, even though he and the man appeared close to the same age, "this ship is supposed to have somewhere close to five thousand people on it. Do you really expect me to believe they're all dead?"

"Look around you, sir," the man argued. "This mess up here is nothing compared to what's waiting for you inside the ship. Everyone, and I mean everyone, is dead. I'm all that's left and if we don't get out of here soon, we'll all be dead too."

"I believe him, sir," Diana spoke up. "Look at him. What reason does he have to lie?"

Lieutenant Page shot Diana a glare that told her to shut her mouth. He was the CO of this OP, not her.

"The sun is setting, sir," Greg added. "And it looks like the ship's backup power just failed. If we go in there, we'll be doing it in the dark."

"Alright," Page conceded, knowing wisdom when he heard it. "We've got ourselves a witness. Let's get him back to the *Peart* and let the commander pick his brain. Spraker can make the call on what to do from there."

"Thank you," the man said to Page as Diana and Greg led him passed the lieutenant towards the edge of the deck where the squads' three boats awaited below.

****

Lex couldn't believe he was alive and safe as he sat in the *Peart*'s briefing room waiting on Commander Spraker to arrive. The *Peart*'s doctor had checked him over. He was malnourished but otherwise okay as far as the doctor could tell. After watching what happened to Trish when one of the things aboard the *Pleasure Bound* had injured her, Lex had been afraid he might be infected with something the creatures had passed on too but all his bloodwork had come back clean. He felt amazing. The long shower he had been allowed made him feel like a new man. Lex felt clean for the first time in days. His hair was still wet when the MPs had escorted him here. He didn't mind waiting on Commander Spraker. Two bottles of water, one already half empty, and a tray of food sat on the table in front of him. Lex was trying to force himself to take things slow but the eggs on the plate were just so freaking good. He shoveled mouthful after mouthful of them into his stomach.

The door opened and Commander Spraker entered. Spraker looked to be his age. Lex had to admit, he had been expecting someone older. He didn't know much about the navy except what he saw on TV and in the movies, but Spraker still struck him as young to be in command of his own ship.

Spraker pulled out the chair across from Lex sat and took a seat.

"I trust you're feeling better, Mr. Iver?" Spraker asked.

Lex beamed at him. "Better than I ever thought I would again."

"Good. I am glad to hear it. However, we need to talk about what happened aboard the *Pleasure Bound*. I realize you've been through a lot these last few days, but it's imperative that we know if whoever murdered your fellow passengers remains a threat to us."

Lex was chewing on another fork full of eggs as he tried to answer. His reply came out muffled and distorted. He paused and swallowed the eggs. "Sorry. I don't think I have ever had eggs as good as these are before."

"Perfectly understandable, Mr. Iver," Spraker said, acknowledging Lex's apology.

"You've got it all wrong, Commander," Lex met Spraker's eyes.

"How so?" Spraker leaned forward in his chair.

"It's not a matter of who, sir. It's a matter of what," Lex told him. "The *Pleasure Bound* wasn't attacked by terrorists or anything like that.

She was attacked by monsters, like something you'd see in your nightmares."

"I don't have nightmares with monsters, Mr. Iver. At least not the sort I assume you're referring to," Spraker said flatly. "I've seen enough horror in this world to know what real monsters are and they're people just like us in that they're flesh and blood. Evil, sadistic, cruel men who prey on the weak. That's what monsters are to me."

"Surely your men must have encountered some of those…things as they were boarding the *Pleasure Bound*," Lex protested.

"You are the only thing we found alive on that ship, Mr. Iver. Just you," Spraker said.

Lex grunted in disbelief. "Well, trust me they were there. There were hundreds of them."

"And what are *they*, Mr. Iver?"

"How in the devil am I supposed to know that?" Lex asked. "If I hadn't seen them myself, I wouldn't believe such things could exist either."

"Tell me about them," Spraker demanded.

"Have you ever seen a squid, Commander?"

Spraker gave Lex an odd look. "I have."

"They were squids, Commander. The things that slaughtered the passengers and crew of the *Pleasure Bound* were squids."

"That's insane," Spraker laughed.

"Yes, Commander, it is. It's true, though. They came out of the water, scaling the sides of the *Pleasure Bound* like messed-up spiders. They swept over her decks, leaving a trail of death in their wake."

"You're being serious?" Spraker stared at Lex.

"I am. Who could make crap like that up?"

"I've read your file, Mr. Iver. You were a horror writer, a rather popular one too, up until the last couple of years."

"Fame comes and goes," Iver shrugged. "But if you're implying that I am trying to spin this into some PR stunt for my work, you're the one who is crazy. My wife died on that cruise liner, Commander. I watched one of those things tear her apart right in front of me."

"I'm sorry for your loss, but even so…"

"Do I really expect you to believe me? Yes, I do, Commander. Someone has to do something about those things before they stumble onto another ship and have it as a follow-up course."

"Follow-up course? Are you being literal?"

"The squids ate the folks aboard that ship, Commander. They were like a swarm of locusts attacking a field. No one on the *Pleasure Bound* stood a chance."

"Squids don't climb, Mr. Iver. They don't eat people either."

"These did," Lex told Spraker.

"So what you're telling me, for the record, Mr. Iver, is that a swarm of mutant squids, who can climb the sides of ships and move about on land like spiders, ate everyone on board the cruise liner we picked up from?"

"I am," Lex answered. "You've got to find those things, Commander, and make sure they never get the chance to do it to another ship again."

"Thank you, Mr. Iver," Commander Spraker said and rose from his seat. "My crew will see to your needs while you're onboard. I regret to inform you though your stay with us may be longer than you might expect. We're in the middle of an operation and not due into port for some time."

"Thank you, Commander," Lex said, smiling. "I'm alive thanks to you and your crew. I think I can manage to survive however long it takes you to get me home."

****

Arron was in a spot that made it clear that he had been listening to the exchange between Mr. Iver and Spraker as the commander emerged from the briefing room.

"Is he for real?" Arron asked.

"Sure seems to be," Spraker frowned.

"Could be that the time alone, trapped below decks, on that ship drove him mad. Not to mention watching that lady splatter her brains all over the wall," Arron suggested.

"How do you know about that?" Spraker asked.

"I overheard the doc telling you when he delivered his report on good Mr. Iver there."

"McHan isn't a psychologist but he did give Iver a clean bill of health," Spraker rubbed at his cheeks with the tips of the fingers of his right hand, thinking, before adding, "You sure overhear a lot."

"Wouldn't be doing my job if I didn't," Arron chuckled.

"I'm not about to call up Captain Marcus and tell him that a swarm of mutated squids ate the people on board that ship, Arron. Not without hard proof anyway."

"Should I send the squads back over? Maybe have them take a second look around now that we know what to look for? I know Page is dying to

KRAKEN

return to that ship. He refuses to believe Iver is the only survivor of a vessel that large."

Spraker took a moment before answering. "No. Not yet anyway. If on the highly unlikely chance Mr. Iver isn't insane, we'd just be putting them in harm's way. There's no need for it at this point. I want Luke to run full sonar scans of the waters around us. Maybe he can turn up something that lends some credence to Iver's story. Oh, and double the lookouts. I want as many eyes on the water as we can spare. Not just to try to confirm Iver's tale, but to make sure nothing sneaks up on us like it did the *Pleasure Bound*."

"Good idea, sir," Arron nodded. "I'll get on that straight away."

"I'll be in my ready room if you need me," Spraker told Arron.

Spraker headed straight to his ready room, leaving Arron to carry out his orders. He trusted Arron to get the things that needed done, done and done well. Besides, he needed time to think. The situation was well outside the realm of anything he had dealt with before. Having Captain Marcus as the CO of DESRON 22 didn't make things any easier.

His mood was not a good one as Spraker entered his ready room. He slammed its door behind him in an attempt to vent some of the frustration built up inside him. He knew the best option was to order the boarding party back to the *Pleasure Bound,* but he just couldn't bring himself to do it. He'd sent men to their deaths before. Facing danger was part of any military officer's job and that went double for marines. . Yet, something inside of him gnawed at his brain, telling him that Lex Iver might not be insane. If Iver's story was true and there were real, living monsters that ate people out there in the water, there was no guarantee that Page and his men would have the firepower to deal with them. Their own disbelief, which Spraker knew would feel just as strongly as he did himself, would also put them at a disadvantage against the monsters if they turned out to be over there, waiting. There were times when a situation demanded the blood of his men, but this wasn't one of them…yet.

Spraker took a seat behind his desk. He wasn't a drinker like a lot of other captains and commanders. His crew, certainly Arron, gave him a lot of flak over that fact. He was a smoker though and dug into the carton of cigarettes he kept in his desk drawer, lighting one up, as he placed an ashtray that was also tucked away in the drawer, onto his desktop. He took a long drag from his cigarette, causing its end to flare from how hard he sucked on it. The nicotine hit him like a hammer. He savored the head rush and the tension he felt eased up a bit. Spraker sat there, smoking cigarette after cigarette, as he mulled things over and tried to come up with what he was really going to tell Captain Marcus. Whatever he told Marcus, he had to do it soon.

A rapid fire, loud knock banged on the door to his ready room startling Spraker. He ground out his cigarette in the ashtray in front of him as he called out, "What is it?"

Arron flung open the door and rushed inside. Arron was pale as he spoke. "Sir, we've lost contact with the main body of DESRON 22."

Spraker leaped to his feet nearly knocking his ashtray to the metal floor at his feet. "What do you mean we've lost contact with the DESRON?"

"I had Megan attempt to contact the *Whiteside*. Our report on the situation here was overdue and I was hoping to stall Marcus and buy you a little more time to come up with your report. You know what a stickler he is about protocol. Well, there was no reply. When I left the bridge, Megan was still trying to contact the *Whiteside* without any luck."

"That doesn't make any sense," Spraker said. "What about the other ships in the DESRON?"

"Only some of the other frigates who were out on patrol are responding, sir. They confirm that they can't raise the main fleet either."

"Dear God help us," Spraker muttered. "Iver may have been telling the truth after all."

II

Captain Marcus sat in the command chair on the USS *Whiteside*'s bridge. He popped the knuckles of his right hand, one after the other. He knew his crew could tell he was on edge. The unexpected appearance of a civilian cruise liner at the edge of borders he assigned to the training exercise DESRON 22 was undergoing was pure madness. There shouldn't have been another ship anywhere close to the area the powers that be had selected for him to run this op. in. Worse, that slacker, Spraker, had yet to report any information he might have obtained about why the bloody cruise liner had happened upon the DESRON. Spraker had been given more than ample time to report something, anything, about the nature of the cruise ship. Yet, all Marcus knew was what he had known since the ship was detected. It was a large passenger liner by the name of the *Pleasure Bound*. It was a long stretch from the course it was supposed to be on and adrift. Spraker had reported having made contact with the cruise liner and some nonsense about how whoever he had spoken with aboard it claiming the massive vessel had been attacked. Marcus figured if the ship had been attacked, it was the work of pirates. A ship like the *Pleasure Bound* surely made a tempting target to the thieves and plunders who made their home in international waters. The thing that bugged him about his assumption was the size of the vessel. It would take an equally large or highly organized group of pirates to pull off such a feat.

His XO had pulled up everything they could get on the cruise liner. A rough guess put the combined number of staff and passengers aboard it at close to five thousand men and women. The ship was of a class that warranted heavy security aboard it. Armed security forces at that likely highly so. Professional officers who knew the dangers these waters could hold and were trained to deal with them.

There had been no distress call from the *Pleasure Bound* before she appeared on the *Peart*'s radar though, according to Spraker. Marcus found that hard to believe. Pirates wouldn't be able to incapacitate such a large population to the point of where no one was able to send out a call after they took whatever they were after and left. The pirates might have disabled the ship's comm. gear to prevent such a call from being made but Spraker had told him the *Peart* had established contact with the cruise liner, however briefly. As thus, that ruled out the pirates disabling the comm. gear because it was still clearly functional. And Marcus refused to believe even terrorists would've killed that many unarmed men and women only to leave the ship behind, much less pirates. No, thinking in those extremes, pirates would have found more value in selling the women and children in the sex slave trade. And they would have kept the ship. One like the *Pleasure Bound* was sure to fetch a huge price as salvage if they could pull that one off. It wouldn't be that hard to do if the pirate had a place to stash her and sit on her for a while.

Marcus stopped cracking his knuckles and picked up the lukewarm cup of tea he had been neglecting from the arm of his chair. He sipped at it as he continued thinking about the mystery of the *Pleasure Bound*. The USS *Whiteside*'s sonar tech, Venkman, interrupted his thoughts.

"Sir," Venkman called to him. "I'm picking up some odd activity in the water."

Marcus cocked his head in Venkman's direction waiting for a further explanation.

"There's something going on with the sea life out there, sir."

"Define something," Marcus gritted his teeth, wishing Venkman would just spit whatever it was out and get it over with.

"The largest shoal of squids I have ever seen, maybe even the biggest one on record, is headed towards DESRON 22, sir. They're approaching at close to twenty knots," Venkman said as if he disbelieved his own report.

"That's impossible," Marcus threw himself forward in his seat. "No squid can move that fast."

"Unless our instruments are in error, these are, sir," Venkman confirmed. "I have tripled checked the data, sir."

"That certainly is strange," Marcus mused. "Not sure it matters to us though. Maybe it's a mass migration or something."

"The squids appear to be on a *direct* course for DESRON 22," Venkman clarified.

"Even so, officer…"

"Venkman, sir. I'm Stanz's replacement. He's in sickbay at the moment with a bad case of stomach flu."

"Officer Venkman, this is a United States destroyer not a science vessel," Marcus reprimanded him. "I appreciate your caution and attention what's going on around us, but this, this might be taking things a touch overboard."

"Yes, sir," Venkman bowed his head respectfully under Marcus's angry stare.

"Forget about the shoal, Venkman. We've got more important things to deal with."

****

Aboard the USS *Peterson,* Captain Clarence Wirtz was having much the same conversation with his own sonar tech, Lee.

"That is one messed-up shoal of squids," Wirtz commented looking over Lee's shoulder at the sonar screen.

"It surely is, sir. Biggest one on record I think." Lee ran a nervous hand through his regulation-cut black hair. "I didn't know what to what to make of it, so I thought you might want to take a look for yourself."

"I'm glad you reported it," Wirtz said, squeezing Lee's shoulder. "What I don't understand about it is why are those things headed straight for DESRON 22? You'd think their instinct would be to steer as far clear of it as they could."

"Agreed, sir." Lee smiled at Captain Wirtz. "If I were a squid, I'd sure as heck want to stay out of the path of something as large as even this ship. And we're not just talking about the *Peterson*. We're talking about four destroyers in battle formation."

Wirtz laughed. "If this is supposed to be a battle formation, our dear Captain Marcus has a lot to learn."

"The DESRON is rather spread out sir but even so…"

"Yeah, I know," Wirtz assured Lee. "We still should be utterly terrifying to a group of squids no matter how large a group it is."

"The shoal's course indicates they're coming straight at us too," Lee reminded him.

"No much we can do about it sailor," Wirtz shrugged. "If we open fire on a group of animals, can you imagine the political mess that would create on the mainland? Besides, they're squids. It's not like they're a threat to us."

"I still don't like it, Captain," Lee admitted.

"Neither do I, son. To tell the truth, that shoal creeps me out. Keep an eye on it for me," Wirtz told Lee and it *was* the truth. He didn't have all the details but he had heard squids mentioned in the comm. chatter between the *Peart* and the *Whiteside.* The snippets he'd overheard weren't to his liking either, and now this supersized shoal of squids showing up out of nowhere just like that cruise ship had, it might be more than mere chance. "If anything changes with it, inform me at once."

"Yes, sir," Lee barked as Wirtz started back to his command chair.

He had barely managed a few steps in its direction when Lee shouted for him.

"Sir, the shoal is breaking apart!" Lee yelled. "It's dividing to target each of the ships in DESRON 22."

"What do you mean targeting, son?" Wirtz kept his voice calm as he spoke.

"The shoal has broken into four distinct groupings, sir. Each is headed for a particular ship of DESRON 22. Their speed has increased too!"

"But you said they were already pushing twenty knots," Wirtz pointed out.

"Yes, sir, I did. They're closer to twenty-five knots now."

"Dear God," Wirtz breathed knowing that such a speed was impossible for squids of the size that appeared to be coming after DESRON 22.

Wirtz whirled around to shout at Charles, his XO. "Inform Captain Marcus about these things at once!" Then he turned back to Lee, "ETA?"

"They're a good bit out, sir, but even so, I'd say four minutes tops."

KRAKEN

"Bring the ship to battle stations!" Wirtz ordered.

"Isn't that a bit extreme, sir?" Charles asked.

The two of them had served together a long time and Wirtz was used to Charles calling him on things that were questionable.

"I'm playing a hunch, Charles. It's on me if I am wrong," Wirtz explained.

Charles gave him a sharp nod, knowing better than to push the issue. "Yes, sir."

"The squids have reached the *Arrington*!" Lee shouted.

****

Captain Holland's sonar tech hadn't been as attentive as those aboard the *Whiteside* and the *Peterson*. The *Emerson* and her crew had no warning of the approaching squids, not that they would have viewed the fast closing shoal as a threat in any case.

Seaman Jenkins was the first to die. He was walking along the starboard side of the ship when a monster came scampering over the railing into his path. His brain didn't even have time to fully process the horror he saw before one of the creature's tentacles lashed out with such force, it caved in his skull like a hammer striking a rotten melon.

Seaman Fleming was several feet behind Jenkins and witnessed his death. He did have time to scream. The squid moved across the deck like a wobbly spider at a speed that was unbelievable. Seaman Fleming had no weapon. He turned to run, but the squid overtook him easily. One of its tentacles pierced his body like a spear, lifting Seaman Fleming from the deck, before it flung his corpse from the ship into the waves below.

Other members of the crew on the higher decks of the USS *Arrington* had more time to react. Most of them ran for whatever doorway leading into the ship's interior they were closest to.

Hundreds of squids swarmed the *Arrington*. The creatures covered the sides of the ship as they used their tentacled clubs to haul their light bodies upwards along the hull and onto the *Arrington*'s decks.

Captain Holland was caught completely off guard by the B-horror movie that was coming alive onboard his ship.

"Sir!" his XO, Weston yelled at him. "We're under attack! I've got reports coming in from all over the ship!"

"Who?" Holland snarled at Weston. "Who is attacking us?"

"Squids, sir," Weston reported. "The men are saying we're being attacked by squids."

"Squids?" Holland repeated the word, making it sound like a curse.

"Mobilize the Security Alert Teams and sound battle stations!" Holland roared.

Alarm klaxons were blaring throughout the *Arrington* as the first reaction team onto the primary deck encountered the army of squids that was building there.

"Good Lord in heaven, have mercy on us!" Harold, the team's leader, muttered as he saw the creatures.

Harold and the men with him opened fire. Harold and his team were armed with M-16s. The rifles chattered spitting three round bursts into the monsters already charging to meet them. One squid jerked about as it took a burst to its central mass. Black blood flew from its twitching body as it careened wildly under the sustained fire Harold poured into it. Finally, it flopped to the deck to lay still. Harold was dead too though.

Another squid had reached his position and tore his face off with a single, lightning-fast swipe of one of its tentacled claws.

Harold's men tried to fall back, but the squids swept over them a like tidal wave of death. A few squids stopped to feed on the bodies of the team, but the bulk of them continued forward.

Commander Les Johnson led two more of the *Arrington*'s Security Alert teams head on towards the things. Johnson lobbed a grenade into the moving mass of limbs in front of him and ducked as it detonated. The explosion filled the air with sticky, black pulp, blowing apart nearly a dozen of the squids. The blast and the death of their brethren didn't even slow the other squids down. They came on like a giant, red juggernaut.

Johnson and his team opened up at them. M-16s chattered. MP9's cracked. Even the occasional thunder of a twelve gauge joined in the cacophony of battle. Squid after squid gave a strange cry of pain that was an inhuman cross between a hiss and shriek as they died, but there was just too many of the things. Johnson watched his men begin to die one by one as the squids reached them. The things didn't just move along the deck, they raced along the walls of the ship as well, their main bodies sticking out sideways with the points of their heads, for lack of a better word, pointed out towards the water.

A squid took a burst of fire as it leapt at him. The burst caught it so close to Johnson that the thing's black blood splattered over him like a putrid rain. He wiped the sticky, slime-like crud from his eyes and face with the backside of his hand, barely bringing his shotgun back up in time to get off a shot at the squid behind it. His shotgun boomed. Its heavy round reduced the squid's main body to a mess of pulp that stained the deck of the ship. Pumping a fresh round into his shotgun's chamber, he heard a man screaming behind him. Johnson cocked his head around to see Ben, one of the NCOs of his squad, being lifted from the deck by the tentacles of two squids. The creatures were having a tug of war with him, or at least they were until Ben's body gave out and ripped in half across his abdomen. One creature got his legs and lower torso while the other got his still-screaming head and the half that went with it.

Johnson spat a litany of curses as he continued to retreat and blew another squid apart. He had only had two rounds left now and there was no time to reload. If he paused to do so, he was dead and he knew it.

Another of his men died as one of the squids flung itself from the wall of the ship onto him and the two of them went toppling over the side railing into the waves below.

"Fall back!" Johnson yelled to the men who were still alive and retreating in the same direction he was. There was nowhere to fallback to though. The direction they were headed only led to more of the squids who had scampered onto the ship's deck between them and the entrance to its interior.

Johnson spent his last round saving one of his men who was pinned to the deck with one of the squids on top of him. He rolled away from the splattered remains of the squid that Johnson's shot had took out only to have the tentacle of another squid close around his neck. Johnson watched as it constricted and popped the man's head from his shoulders. The man's head rolled along the deck to disappear beneath the tentacles of a fresh mass of squids that was closing in fast.

Fishing a handful of rounds from his pocket, Johnson tried to shove one into his shotgun's chamber. It went flying from his hand as tentacle slammed into his back and knocked him from his feet. His shotgun went bouncing from his hands as he hit the deck so hard he felt the air leave his lungs. Struggling to breathe, Johnson ripped his MP9 from the holster on his hip and brought it up at the squid that stood over him. The thing's stance reminded him for a picture he had seen in an old paperback of H.G. Wells' War of the Worlds. Its two main tentacles or arms slashed madly over him as it stood on the others.

The MP9 barked over and over again as Johnson emptied half its magazine, point blank, into the creature. The squid gave a squeal that sounded like air streaming out of a leaking tire and jumped out of his line of fire. Its powerful limbs sent it soaring to land several yards from where it had been.

Johnson hurled himself to his feet, popping off two rounds at another squid that dove at him from his right. The rounds met the squid head-on and explosions of black blood erupted into the air from where they dug into its body. They weren't enough to stop the creature's momentum though, and only seemed to tick it off more before it collided with him.

The squid's weight wasn't enough to take Johnson down again, though. Instead, he found himself with the creature wrapped about his body as its many arms slithered and slashed over him. Each arm left bright trails of red and torn flesh in its wake as it tightened around him, but that pain was nothing compared to the thing's beak. It was pressed against his stomach where he could feel it ripping away chunks of him. Purple, red-soaked strands of intestines bulged from the wounds the beak tore in him. Johnson gave one last cry of pain before his world went dark and his life was over.

On the *Arrington*'s bridge, Captain Holland and his XO stared at the ship's forward window. One minute there had been the view of the blue sky and the water ahead of the ship, the next there was nothing but red. A mass of moving, writhing bodies covered it. Tentacles whipped up against the thickened glass trying to break through it.

The squids were already onboard the *Arrington* so her weapons were useless against them.

Communications Officer Delores Fagan was doing her best to let the other ships of DESRON 22 know what was happening aboard the *Arrington* when suddenly she looked up from her console and screamed, "The comm. is down, sir! Those things must have taken out the transmitters!"

The forward window of the *Arrington*'s bridge was beginning to fracture. Tiny spiderweb-like cracks ran up and down its surface.

"Everyone off the bridge!" Weston shouted, heading for the door himself.

Captain Holland stood, paralyzed, partly from fear and partly from the awe he felt of the sight in front of him as he watched the mass of squids pressed up against the window.

"Sir!" Weston called but Holland didn't hear him. He was entirely focused on the squids.

Then the window caved inward…

The squids managed to get into the *Arrington*'s interior by any way they could: broken windows, left open bulkheads, it didn't matter so long as they were able to continue pursuing their prey. And despite the hastily handed out weapons from the ship's stores, her sailors were just that — prey.

****

Captain Marcus was in shock as his XO told him again, "Sir, we've lost all contact with the *Arrington.*"

Marcus shook his head, clearing it. "I heard you the first time," he growled.

"The squids appear to have come out of the water, sir, scaling the sides of her hull, and engaging the *Arrington*'s Security Alert Teams."

"The squids are closing on us too, sir!" Venkman informed Marcus. "ETA less than two minutes!"

"Evasive maneuvers!" Marcus snapped. "Full military power!"

Marcus knew it was too little, too late. A ship the size of the *Whiteside* would never be able to turn about and gain enough speed before creatures as fast and agile in the water as the squids could move.

"Battle stations! Bring the ship's CIWS online!" Marcus's XO added.

The CIWS came instantly to life as soon as the parameters of its target were uploaded. One gun fired then another. Each pumped five thousand rounds a minute into the waves around the *Arrington* as she veered about in the water. The water grew black and thick around her hull.

"Sir!" his XO shouted. "I have reports of the squids boarding us on the portside!"

"Scramble all the Security Alert teams!" Marcus ordered. "We can't allow them to gain a foothold or we're as dead as the *Arrington*!"

"Yes, sir!" his XO barked before moving to carry out the order.

****

Captain Wirtz had already ordered the *Peterson*'s helmsman to bring her about and bring her to full speed as the carnage aboard the *Arrington* was taking place. He knew he should have waited for Captain Marcus's order to do so, but he'd be damned if he was going to sit back and watch his men die. Wirtz was glad he had made that call. Those on the *Peterson*'s bridge had heard the howls and desperate cries for help over the open comm. channel to the *Arrington* until those cries had suddenly been replaced by silence and the crackle of dead air.

Every officer Wirtz could spare was busy raiding the ship's stores and passing out weapons to anyone who would take one. Wirtz's Security Alert Teams were already on the *Peterson*'s primary decks too, armed to the teeth, and well aware of what might be coming at them if Wirtz's actions weren't enough to get the large ship clear in time.

Sargent Wike, the CO of the ship's topside defenders, gritted his teeth as he looked over the railing at the mass of swarming red in the water to the *Peterson*'s portside. So far, that mass was remained a good distance away, but he knew that could change in a heartbeat. He pumped his twelve gauge, chambering a round. At this point, all he could do was wait and a mumble a prayer.

Wirtz had also stationed detachments of the ship's marines at other key points inside her. Engineering and the entrances to the bridge were guarded by veteran killers like Wike, equally ready to face whatever came at them.

"Any word from the *Whiteside?*" Wirtz asked his comm. officer.

"None, sir," came the quick response.

Sonar Tech Lee motioned for Wirtz and Charles' attention. "Sir! The *Emerson*! She's gone, sir!"

Wirtz and Charles rushed towards the sonar station to join Lee at his post.

"Those squids overrun her too?" Charles asked.

"I wouldn't bet on that, Charles. Davis is one sharp cookie. If they got her, they didn't do it without a fight," Wirtz said.

Lee was frantically shaking his head. "No, sir, you don't understand. The *Emerson* is gone. She's not on my screen anymore."

Wirtz's eyebrows rose in confusion. "What do you mean she's not there?"

"Something the size of a naval frigate doesn't just disappear, son," Charles said so angrily that spittle flew from his lips as he spoke.

"One second, she was there in formation and the next she was just gone. Check for yourself, sir. There's no sign of her," Lee protested.

"What in the devil is that?" Charles asked, his finger stabbing a large dot on the screen that was close to the position where the *Emerson* should have been.

"Whatever it is, it isn't anything good," Wirtz told Charles. "That thing is almost a time and a half larger than the *Whiteside*... And it's moving."

"You don't think..." Charles stammered.

"Another shoal even larger than the first one?" Wirtz asked.

"I don't think so, sir," Lee told them both. "That thing is solid."

"All the more reason to get out of here as fast as we can," Wirtz concluded. "I, for one, don't want to find out what it is the hard way."

"Agreed," Charles nodded.

"What about the *Emerson*?" Lee asked.

"She's on her own," Wirtz said, trying not to sound too cold. He liked Davis, liked her a lot actually, but this war and it was "every man for himself" time if there ever was one. "Is that detachment for the main shoal still closing on us?"

Lee nodded. "We're up to around twenty-eight knots and pouring on all we can, sir. They're pulling about twenty nine as of now."

"We've got a head start on those things at least," Charles commented. "That's more than the others had."

"How long until they overtake us?" Wirtz squeezed Lee's shoulder.

"At present speeds, we've stretched the original four minutes we had to over ten, sir. More if we continue to gain speed as quickly as we have been," Lee answered.

Wirtz whirled about on his weapons officer. "Can we get a firing solution on them without endangering the other ships of the DESRON?"

The *Peterson*'s weapons officer was a middle-aged, snaggle-toothed fellow named Melton. He cocked his head as he appeared to mull over Wirtz's question. "Does that include the *Arrington,* sir?"

"Yes. It does." Wirtz wished it didn't. "She may be lost but there might still be sailors alive on her in her lower decks."

"It'd be difficult but I think I can manage it," Melton shrugged.

"Do it," Wirtz ordered. "Take the detachment of squids pursuing us under guns and get a lock on them. Fire at will."

The *Peterson* wasn't truly equipped for sub-warfare. Most of her weapons were geared towards surface and airborne enemies, but like most of the new ships of the DESRON, she also sported hull-mounted torpedo launchers. She only had four, two aft facing, and two forward.

Wirtz watched nervously as Melton acquired his target and fired. Both of the aft launchers put torpedoes in the water. They streaked under the waves to intercept the mass of squids in pursuit of the *Peterson.* The water spouted upwards towards the sky in black tinted geysers above the point where they made contact with the mass of squids.

"Torpedoes one and two are both direct hits, sir!" Lee shouted excitedly.

Wirtz didn't blame the sonar tech for his outburst. It was about time DESRON 22 drew some blood in return for the loss of the *Arrington* and the *Emerson.* Each ship had upwards of a hundred members of crew on them and if they weren't already dead, the odds were they would be before the day was through. Wirtz held out hope that there were crewmen left alive aboard the *Arrington* and fighting to remain so until help could reach them. Sadly, he had no means of doing so at the present time. The DESRON had no carrier in its ranks. Only the *Whiteside* was carrying any a bird. A Seawolf rested on her helipad. The *Whiteside,* though, wasn't in any position to launch her. Odds are she was as overrun as the *Arrington* by now. There had been no word from Captain Marcus since the shoal's original separation and engagement of the DESRON.

He really wanted to blame Captain Marcus for all the souls death had already claimed today, but just couldn't bring his self to do it. No one, really no one, could have seen something like what the DESRON was facing now coming.

Wirtz knew his best hope of helping the men aboard the *Arrington*, if indeed there were any left alive, was to get the heck out of here and return when the main shoal of squids had moved on. If the events aboard that cruise liner were an indication, they would move on after they fed.

"We're pulling ahead of the squids, sir!" Lee added somehow managing to sound even more excited. "The torpedoes must have done a lot of damage to them. If I am reading my screen correctly, the size of the sub-shoal in pursuit of us has been reduced in size by almost forty percent."

"We're not out of the woods yet," Charles pointed reminded him as Wirtz moved to sit in his command chair.

"No, we're not," Wirtz agreed. "Have we been able to get a message to command back home and let them know what's happening out here?"

Charles shook his head. "Something is interfering with the long-range comms."

"Figures," Wirtz snorted.

Charles laughed. "Could be worse."

"Worse than being chased by a pack of men-eating squids which have already taken out two of our destroyers and most likely a third as well?" Wirtz challenged him. "Tell me, how does it get worse than that?"

"Could be a pack of Megalodons," Charles joked in an attempt to break the tension everyone on the *Peterson*'s bridge was feeling.

Wirtz couldn't help it. He laughed at that the joke despite the mess they were in.

"Okay, I'll give you that one," he conceded with a wry grin.

"Lee, what's the status of the unknown contact near the *Emerson*'s last known position?" Wirtz asked.

"It's gone, sir," Lee said, again sounding as if he didn't believe his own report.

Wirtz let out a frustrated sigh. "Of course it is."

"Mr. Melton, if you would, please take the approaching detachment of squids under guns again and give them one more reason why they don't want to keep following us."

"Yes, sir!" Melton answered with perhaps a bit too much mad glee in his voice. "Tubes 3 and 4, torpedoes away!"

The second volley almost finished the detachment of squids trailing the *Peterson* entirely. Lee reported that what remained of them broke up into smaller groups and changed course, giving up their pursuit.

"Looks like that did it," Charles smiled.

"Maybe," Wirtz said. "We still need to get clear of whatever is causing the interference with the long-range comms. We have to get a message out and let command know about what's happening here. There are sailors aboard the *Arrington* and the *Whiteside* who are likely in dire need of help that we ourselves are in no position to render."

"Sir," Lee called to Wirtz. "I've got that large contact back on my screen!"

"Position and heading?" Wirtz asked keeping his tone calm.

"It's under us, sir," Lee said.

Wirtz frowned just before the *Peterson* lurched around him. He could hear the metal of her hull bending inward and straining against some outside pressure that was being applied to it as he was thrown from his seat to topple head first to the deck.

Charles was flung across the bridge. He struck the forward wall with the sickening, snapping sound of breaking bones.

Lee screamed as the sonar station erupted in flames and blew out in front of him. He leaped from his seat, the arms of his uniform ablaze and his features twisted into a grotesque visage of pain.

Part of the bridge ceiling collapsed and tumbled downwards onto the helm. The helmsman threw himself away from his station just in time to avoid being crushed, only to bash his head so hard on the deck that blood leaked from the corners of his mouth where he lay unconscious only a few feet from Wirtz.

The last thing Wirtz saw before he died was the view of a tentacle too large to put into words through the *Peterson*'s forward bridge window as it came crashing down onto the ship.

****

Commander Spraker's worry about DESRON 22's situation turned to panic as he read over the reports Arron had given him. They weren't as detailed as he was would have liked but that wasn't Arron's or anyone else's fault among his crew. There had been no direct communications between the *Peart* and the main body of DESRON 22, but his comm. officer, Megan, had managed to get the comm. back online from whatever the sudden, out of nowhere interference that had stuck it to catch bits and pieces of DESRON 22's final moments. And yes, if what the reports contained were even half true, DESRON 22 was gone, at least its main body of destroyers at any rate. The *Peart* had managed to make contact with two of the other frigates on patrol, one of which belonged to his friend, Cordova.

It seemed that lunatic, Iver, they had rescued from the adrift civilian cruise ship, the *Pleasure Bound*, was telling the truth after all. Spraker found himself wishing the man had just been as stark, raving mad as his claims about what happened on that ship made him sound. That wasn't the case though. The reports on his desk confirmed that DESRON 22, or rather what remained of it, was indeed facing a shoal of rampaging, mutated, carnivorous squids.

Spraker looked up from the reports as a knock rang out on the door to his ready room.

"Come," he called.

The door opened to reveal a rather worried-looking Arron.

"You've read the reports then?" he asked, noticing Spraker's paleness and grim expression.

"I have," Spraker said. "I don't want to believe them but I do. Part of me wants to think this is all some elaborate prank Cordova cooked up with Captain Marcus to pay me back for not being the commander Marcus thinks I should be. I know the two of them would be lucky to be in the same room for any amount of time without Cordova ending up in the brig."

"I know what you mean," Arron said as he took a seat in the empty chair in front of Spraker's desk. "It all reminds of me of a really great horror film I saw when I was young. I can't remember the exact title but it was called Deep… something or other. Man, I loved that movie."

"I'm not really up for being a part of a real life horror film, Arron. Sorry, but I'd like to see my wife again."

Arron nodded. "We're in pretty deep crap, aren't we?"

"And on our own too from the look of things." Spraker's frown grew. "With the main body of the DESRON gone, that leaves me of all people in command of what's left."

"Well, at least we don't have to put up with Captain Marcus anymore."

Spraker felt anger surge through him. He wanted to punch in Arron's teeth but managed to contain himself, if only just. "Too many good men and woman have died today to make a joke like that, Arron."

"Sorry," Arron offered, turning his eyes to the office's floor.

"It's hard to believe freaking squids took out a DESRON, I know. Trust me. I am sort of in denial over that too, Arron. Everything we have points to that fact, though. It sounds like the *Arrington* was taken out fast too. Once those things got on her, it was over."

"We don't have a real clear picture of what happened to the other destroyers, though," Arron said.

"True," Spraker admitted. "Still, I think it's safe to assume they were taken out in the same manner. The squids came in hard and fast, boarded them, and worked their way through the destroyers like they did on the *Pleasure Bound.*"

Spraker sat the folder of reports that was in his hand onto the top of his desk. "I want to make sure that doesn't happen to us. I want everyone, and I mean everyone, but Mr. Iver, armed as of yesterday. See if the chief can rig up anything to help protect the more critical portions of the *Peart* too. Welding the bulk of the exterior entrances closed wouldn't be a bad idea either."

"I've already got us at battle stations," Arron nodded, "but those ideas sound like really good ones too. I'll get right on them."

"Did you send word to Cordova and Mills?"

Arron nodded again. "Just like you ordered. They're both on their way here to meet up with us. I have to ask, though; do you think concentrating us all in one spot like that is the best way to go?"

"Safety in numbers," Spraker stood up, walking around his desk.

"That didn't help the destroyers," Arron reminded him.

"True, but they were caught entirely with their pants down facing an enemy that has no right to even exist," Spraker countered. "We know what we're dealing with now and have at least some vague notions of how to deal with it."

"I know you don't want to hear this, but Mr. Iver may be useful to us," Arron looked at Spraker who was now standing beside where he sat.

"Whether I like the man or not doesn't matter. Am I willing to admit he's not crazy? Sure. That doesn't make him an expert on these squids, though. He's a horror writer for goodness sake."

"Exactly," Arron shifted about nervously. "He's used to thinking outside the box *and* he just spent the last few days out thinking those things on the *Pleasure Bound*. No one else on that ship lived through it all except for him."

Spraker rubbed at his cheeks. "You always have to have a point, don't you?"

"Pardon me saying so, sir, but now you're beginning to sound like my wife." Arron smiled as he seemed to realize that Spraker knew he was onto something.

"Okay," Spraker said. "You get the things I told you going. I want them completed ASAP. In the meantime, I'll pay Mr. Iver another visit."

****

Lex found himself back onboard the *Pleasure Bound*. His mind told him he had to be dreaming but that didn't make it any less frightening. The red glow of the cruise liner's emergency lights lit the corridor he stood in. The corridor around him was empty. Its walls were smeared with blood and stagnate pools of water stretched across the floor. They weren't deep, barely touching the tops of his shoes. The air was cold and Lex shivered, crossing his arms over his chest to rub himself.

Everything was so quiet. It was like the ship itself had died and he was taking a stroll through its decaying body. The ship certainly smelt like it was rotting. Lex knew the smell really belonged to the corpses and pieces of the men and women the squids had torn apart in their frenzy, but thinking the smell came from the ship made it easier to deal with somehow. So many had died here, families on vacation, lovers on romantic getaways, men and women fleeing their old lives in search of a new start, all of them murdered…eaten by things that shouldn't exist.

Lex splashed through the puddle along the corridor as he tried to find somewhere to hide. There was no sign of the squids but he knew they were here. It was almost as if he could feel them, hiding in the shadows, waiting for the perfect moment to swoop in and take him. Staying out in the open wasn't an option if he wanted to continue living.

He recognized the deck he was on as the command deck of the ship. That meant he was close to the bridge and the room where Trish had taken her own life before his eyes. There had been no reason for her to do so he kept telling himself. The boarding parties from the US Naval frigate, the *Peart,* were already onboard and fanned out on the *Pleasure Bound*'s main exterior deck. All they had to do was make it to them and they could escape, leaving this floating tomb behind them forever. The medical staff aboard the *Peart* could have surely helped Trish. Unlike him, they were trained professionals. He was just a horror writer who had picked up a lot of various things from his research over the years of his career. Trish hadn't seen it that way, though. He didn't know if it was the pain from her wounds or her fear that made her splatter her brains all over the wall of the captain of the *Pleasure Bound*'s office. He suspected the later. He should have never handed her the pistol but it was hers and at the time, he hadn't even considered her doing something so *stupid*. A part of him hated Trish for it. Taking one's own life was a cowardly and selfish thing to do.

Her wounds had come from one of the squids mangling her right wrist and the tiny claw-like hooks that lined its arms, or legs, or whatever you called them, shredding the flesh of her lower thighs. The wounds were bad but not lethal. It was the sickness that was born of them that scared Trish so much. She had a fever from them in less than an hour. It was a bad one too that only seemed to grow hotter with each passing minute.

He thought about her suicide as he approached the room where it had happened. The captain's office was the only open room he could see up ahead of him and only the bridge lay behind. There was one of the squids lurking in the flooded bridge section of the ship. The same one that had hurt Trish so badly and nearly claimed him as its prey. Only the grace of God had allowed the two of them to escape it. He was beginning to remember more and more about Trish's last moments as he neared the room. The details of what she looked like as she pressed the barrel of her pistol to her temple and pulled its trigger were rushing back into his mind. Maybe his mind had blocked them out before but he remembered so much more now in this nightmare world.

As he reached the doorway to the captain's office, Lex paused. He didn't want to go into it, but he could hear the squid on the bridge at the other end of the corridor moving through the water there. If it was getting ready to come after him, he didn't have a choice. It was either go on inside or be standing alone and unarmed in the middle of the corridor when the squid entered it. There was nowhere else to hide.

Taking a deep breath and steeling himself, he stepped into the room. Trish's body lay exactly where he had left it...only it wasn't really Trish anymore. The body in front of him didn't even look fully human. The hand that still clutched the gun that had taken Trish's life was now a curved and twisted tentacle. Its hook hung against the pistol's trigger. Her left arm had grown thicker and was covered in a thick slime-like substance. It appeared to be undergoing some kind of change too. Trish's skin was purple, not the purple of death but a middle shade of color between that of human flesh and the red covering of a squid's body. Six more limbs punctured the sides of her clothes, dangling from her slouched form to the room's floor. Her lips were gone, replaced a tipped bone like formation that grew outwards from her face like a bird's beak.

Lex felt his bladder release itself. Warm liquid ran down the length of his legs, adding the wetness of his already water-logged pants and shoes. He stood there staring at the thing that had once been Trish as it lifted its head towards him. Bright yellow eyes glowed in the dimness of the ship's emergency lighting. They were full of hunger and hatred.

The beak on Trish's face opened to emit a screeching half hiss, half squeal as she rose to her feet. The new limbs lining the sides of her body thrashed about wildly in the air around her.

Lex turned to run but slammed into the side of the office's doorway. His head clanged against the metal there and his world went black.

****

A scream echoed in his quarters aboard the *Peart* as Lex jerked awake, sitting bolt upright in his bed. His skin and the covers of his bed were soaked in sweat. His breath came in ragged gasps as he realized he was safe and started trying to breathe again. The nightmare still had its claws in him as he rolled out of bed and headed for the shower. He checked and doubled checked that was nothing waiting inside it for him before he entered it. The hot water streaming over his skin helped him to shake off most of the darkness that lingered in his mind. He stayed in the shower until his skin was wrinkled and red. Finally, he stepped out and dried himself.

He had no clothes of his own. He hoped the ship's medical staff had burned the ones he had come aboard the *Peart* in. They were little more than rags by that time anyway. The XO of the *Peart,* a good-natured fellow by the name of Arron, had given him a sailor's uniform to wear and Lex was thankful for it. It wasn't much to look at by Lex's standards, but it beat running around the ship naked. Lex wished it had come with a gun included along with the shirt, pants, and shoes but it hadn't.

Even here, on a state of the art naval frigate, Lex had to admit to himself that he didn't really feel safe. He had seen what the squids could do and while he trusted the crew of the *Peart* to do all they could to keep both him and themselves safe, the ocean was the squids' home. It belonged to them. The creatures had the home field advantage and Lex wasn't sure anything would be enough to stop them if they came calling on the *Peart* in force.

Lex sat down the bed to tie his shoes as a knock sounded on the door to his quarters. He hurriedly finished with his shoes and went to answer it. Arron stood in the corridor outside his quarters. Lex's eyes bugged as he saw what Arron held in his hands. It was a well-read copy of *Demons of Night.*

Arron blushed slightly as he saw Lex recognize the book. "Yeah, Mr. Iver, I'm a fan. I started reading your books right before that terrible movie adaptation of *Terror in the Woods* was released."

Lex's lips curled into an expression of disgust at the mention of the movie.

"I don't blame you for that movie, sir," Arron said quickly. "That's just Hollywood. They like to take great books and turn them into utter crap."

Lex laughed and it felt good. He couldn't remember the last time he had.

Arron shoved the copy of *Demons of Night* at him.

"I was hoping you might sign this for me," Arron beamed.

"You and the crew of this ship saved my life," Lex said. "It would be my sincere pleasure to do so."

Arron handed Lex a pen too. As Lex scrawled his name across the book's title page, Arron spoke again.

"I didn't just stop by to get this signed, though. I wanted to let you know that Commander Spraker is coming to pay you another visit. There are some things he'd like to talk to you about in more detail."

Lex heard the worry in Arron's voice. "Is everything okay?"

"Not my place to say, sir," Arron told him as Lex handed the book back to him. "Thanks for this, though. I hope when all this is over, you'll keep writing. You're too good to just quit."

"Who told you I was quitting?"

"Nobody," Arron said. "I just figured that movie must have hurt you a lot, sir. I know it would have me in your place. And I don't mean just emotionally either."

Lex shrugged. "It is what is and at least I got paid."

"That's always a good thing, sir." Arron grinned and then headed on down the corridor holding tight to his newly signed book.

Lex watched him go and thought about Mary. Could he keep writing without her? How was he going to even live much less write without her at his side?

Closing the door to his quarters, Lex took a seat on the edge of its bed to wait on Commander Spraker to arrive. He was glad Lex had told him the commander was coming, but this second visit stunk of trouble. There was no reason for it as far as he could see unless something had happened to prompt it.

Lex didn't have to wait long until a second knock rapped on his door. He opened it to see a haggard-looking Commander Spraker staring back at him.

"Commander," Lex nodded. "I've been expecting you."

Spraker snorted. "Arron told you I was coming, didn't he?"

Lex ignored the question and moved from the doorway, ushering Commander Spraker inside.

"I hear you have some more questions for me. That's good because I have some of my own for you as well."

Commander Spraker cocked an eyebrow at that. "Oh really?"

"Yes, Commander," Lex said, sitting on the edge of the room's bed again. "I want to know what's happening out there. Have you found the squids?"

"I haven't exactly been hunting for them," Spraker remained standing as there was nowhere else to sit.

"That's not an answer," Lex frowned.

"You really want to know?"

"I wouldn't ask if I didn't, Commander."

"They found us," Spraker admitted. "As I mentioned, DESRON 22 was in the middle of a shakedown maneuver when we stumbled onto the cruise liner you were aboard. The *Peart* was on patrol along with the DESRON's other frigates. Since we picked you up, we've lost contact with the main body of the squadron."

"The destroyer and carrier?" Lex asked.

"DESRON 22 doesn't have a carrier assigned to it. It's composed of four destroyers and six frigates."

"You're telling me a rather disturbing amount of information for me being a civilian, Commander. I must say it concerns me as to why you feel the need to do so."

Spraker remained silent for a moment, too long a moment for Lex's liking.

"You've haven't just lost contact with the squadron's main body have you? It's more than that or you wouldn't be here."

Spraker cracked the knuckles of his right hand. "No. You're right. It's more than that. Does that make you feel smart? That you can figure so much without me telling you?"

Lex shrugged. "I'm not an idiot, Commander. I used to write about situations like the one we find ourselves in out here all the time. If I had to guess, the main body of the DESRON was attacked by the squids and destroyed."

"You'd be right too," Spraker growled.

"So you've come to me of all people for advice on what to do next?"

Spraker shook his head. "No, I've come to you to see what you can tell me about the squids. You were trapped on that ship with those things for days. Surely you had to learn something about them during that time."

"Not as much as you're hoping for, I am sure," Lex sighed.

"What else can you tell me about them, Mr. Iver?"

"They're fast. They can move about on land, though they're slower there. They're hungry. And most of all that you never want to see one of them up close."

"You pretty much told me all that during our first talk, Mr. Iver."

"Yes, I did, Commander, but you weren't listening then. Not really. You thought I had gone insane from the trauma of what I had been through on the *Pleasure Bound.*"

"Can you blame for me that, Mr. Iver?"

"No, I can't. I'd likely have thought the same in your place."

Lex stood up and started pacing. "I can tell you that their bodies are soft. They're not hard to kill if you have a good enough weapon. A shotgun would blow one of them apart. An individual squid remains very deadly due to its speed and the strength of its limbs, but their real power comes in their numbers. When they boarded the *Pleasure Bound,* there were hundreds of the things, maybe thousands. Even if the entire population of the cruise liner had been armed, I am not sure we could have beaten them back."

"Not even if you had warning that they were coming?"

Lex grunted. "Maybe then. I don't know. You're the military officer. I am just a writer. What do I know about defending a ship in real life?"

"You being a writer is exactly why I am talking with you again, Mr. Iver," Spraker told him. "Your sort has a tendency to think outside the box and come up with some crazy crap us normal folks would never remotely think of."

"I'm not sure if that was a compliment or an insult," Lex chuckled.

"Take it as the latter in this case, Mr. Iver."

"Please stop calling me that. My name is Lex."

"Whatever you say, Lex." Spraker gave him a mock bow and then turned serious again. "I need to know if you have any idea where those things came from. How many of them you think there might be out there?"

"Again, I am just a writer not a marine biologist. Like I said, there were perhaps a thousand or more them when they hit the *Pleasure Bound*. I have no means to know if they were part of a larger group or the only group of those things out there in the water."

"Assume that the group that hit the *Pleasure Bound* wasn't the only one," Spraker pressed him.

"Even so, they couldn't be a normal occurrence out here or somebody would have stumbled onto them before now. If they've been hitting ships for a while, someone would have had to manage to escape at some point and told the world about their existence. I think it's best to assume they're new to these waters."

"Great," Spraker said his voice dripping with sarcasm. "That still doesn't tell us where they came from or how many there are."

Lex stopped his pacing and looked the commander square in the eye. "I have a theory but you're not going to like it."

Spraker glared at him waiting for Lex to continue.

"These things just woke up," Lex said. "That's my theory."

"Woke up?" Spraker asked as if he still thought Lex was crazy.

"Yes, woke up. Their species was dormant on the ocean floor and something, whether manmade or natural, happened that brought them out of their slumber."

"Is that really possible?"

"Oh yes. I've read about many species like that," Lex lied knowing the commander didn't have a clue either. "The real question is, are they adults?"

"What?" Spraker spat. "What's that even supposed to mean?"

"Exactly what it sounds like, Commander," Lex kept his eyes locked on Spraker's. "The squids we've seen so far are acting as if they're immature. At least that's my take on them. I'd wager somewhere out there in the water is a mother or father, perhaps both, that we haven't seen yet. Perhaps it was the mother that woke up and when she did so, she released her young to feed."

"Are you really suggesting that these monsters that appear to have wiped out a fleet of state of the art American destroyers are just children?"

Lex nodded. Spraker stared at him for a long moment.

"And if these things are children?" Spraker asked.

"Then you can imagine how large the parents must be, Commander," Lex said, his voice dark and cold.

****

Cordova's frigate, the *Rogue,* was the first to arrive at the *Peart*'s position. Mills and his ship, the *Drake,* arrived half an hour later. By the time his two fellow commanders had come aboard the *Peart,* Spraker was almost driven mad by his own impatience. Time was not anyone's friend right now except maybe the squids. Every minute that ticked by was another that the squids might locate the three frigates in and none of them could afford for that to happen yet. There was still no word from any one of ships in the DESRON's main fleet that might have survived their encounter with the squids, nor was there any word from the other three frigates that had been out on patrol like the ones gathered around the *Peart*. The only safe thing for Spraker to do was to write them off and assume that they were destroyed in action as well.

Despite being the first to arrive, Cordova somehow managed to be the last of the commanders to show up for the joint planning session. Spraker and Mills were waiting on in the *Peart*'s briefing room for him when he did finally show. Spraker had daydreams of cutting Cordova's heart out with a spoon while he had been waiting but upon seeing Cordova, those dark thoughts took flight. All he could manage were the words, "You're late, Commander."

"Good to see you too, Spraker," Cordova grinned at him. "I hear the crap has really hit the fan on this one."

"That's an understatement if there ever was one," Mills snapped. "We don't have time for your usually crap, Cordova. It's time you grew up and started acting like the officer you are."

"Hey now!" Cordova started but Spraker cut him off.

"Take a seat, Cordova," Spraker ordered him. "We've got a lot to work out."

"How does it feel to be in charge for once?" Cordova asked Spraker as he took his seat at the table.

"Like the whole world is resting is on my shoulders," Spraker sighed. "That's not why we're all here though. Those things out there have apparently engaged and destroyed all the other ships of DESRON 22. If we want to make it out of these waters alive, gentlemen, we need to get our act together and come up with a plan of how we're going to do that. Between us, we have three frigates. There were four destroyers in the DESRON's main fleet. I'd say that tells us pretty plainly that the odds are not in our favor."

"I read the report you had sent over on these squids," Cordova leaned forward. "They seem to feed and move on. What makes you so sure that they're still even in this area?"

"Because we are," Spraker said. "They're not going to let an easy meal get away from them, Cordova, and that's exactly what we are, an easy meal."

"Agreed," Mills chimed in. "I've had my crew implement the same precautions you've taken here on the *Peart,* Spraker. Everyone is armed and we've welded almost all the exterior entrances closed. I've got my sonar tech constantly sweeping the ocean for signs of the squids as well."

"But it doesn't seem enough, does it?" Spraker nodded. "I know. We need to do something more. We know based on what Mr. Iver has told us that the squids can be taken out by small arm's fire and rather easily too if one is using something with the blast power of a shotgun. Their bodies are soft, so even a MP9 is going to hurt them. I think the trick is going to be not letting them overrun us. Maybe we could set up some .50 cal emplacements along the decks?"

"What we need to do is hightail it out of these waters at maximum military power until either these things are so far behind us they're just a bad memory or our engines burnout from trying," Cordova told them.

"I'm not sure just running like that is in our best interest," Mills argued. "Most predators see running as a sign of weakness and it just urges them on like a ringing dinner bell. I, for one, think we look weak enough already."

"Agreed," Spraker nodded. "That said, we do need to plot a course out of here and get moving, just not so fast as to draw more attention to our ships than is needed."

"Let them come," Cordova said. "My boys on the *Rogue* are ready for them. Who ever heard of running from a shoal of squids anyway? We're navy officers, man. We should be prepping to engage those bastards not running from them."

Mills ignored Cordova, focusing his attention on Spraker. "The sooner we get underway, the better. We do need a plan to engage them too, though. As we've already established, it's unlikely those monsters are just going to let us leave without making a move against us."

"I hear you have a horror writer onboard," Cordova cut in rudely, his laughter echoing off the room's walls, before Spraker could reply to Mills. "What's he think of all this? From I hear, he managed to see them face to face and live through it."

"Mr. Iver is a civilian and his opinion has no bearing in this meeting," Mills protested at once.

"Holy crap!" Cordova laughed again. "The horror writer you have is Lex Iver? The guy that wrote that terrible movie *Terror in the Woods* or whatever it was called?"

"I have questioned Mr. Iver extensively about his time trapped aboard the *Pleasure Bound.* I can assure you that if he were part of this meeting, he would be urging us to run as well," Spraker said, fed up with Cordova's attitude but managing to stay calm. He didn't remember Cordova being such a jerk before but then up until now, he hadn't been the man's commanding officer either. Maybe Captain Marcus had a point about Cordova's competence as an officer after all.

"What else did Mr. Iver have to say about these monsters?" Cordova asked. "Does he know where they all came from?"

"Mr. Iver has a theory regarding that, yes," Spraker said, "But we're not here to debate the origin of the squids, we're here to figure out a means to get out of this mess alive. Don't make me remind you again, Commander Cordova." The warning in his voice was clear or at least Spraker hoped it was. Cordova could be very dense sometimes, though. He prayed this wasn't one of them. The two of them had been friends for a long time and Spraker had no desire to toss Cordova in the brig, though he would if it came down to that. Appointing a new acting CO to the *Rogue* would be problematic, yes, but it was well within his power to do so given the nature of the current circumstances and his own role as acting surface community captain.

"Boy, the power sure went to your head fast, old buddy," Cordova smirked and then immediately drew himself into a more respectful posture. "Whatever you say though, sir."

"Good," Spraker said though he wasn't convinced that Cordova really meant to behave himself. "I want the *Rogue* to take the same precautions that the *Peart* and the *Drake* already have. They may not seem like much, but they could make the difference of life and death if those squids show up."

"Yes, sir," Cordova said, "Consider it done. I'll radio my crew as soon as this meeting is done. They can get things started before I even make it back."

"Anyone got any other ideas?" Spraker pleaded.

Both Cordova and Mills were silent.

"Okay then," Spraker said, getting up. "We'll set course out of here and proceed slowly. In the meantime, I want the sonar tech on each of our ships pumped full of caffeine, if need be, and as alert as possible. Any warning we have of the squids' approach is better than none."

Spraker remained in the briefing room after the other two commanders had left to head back to their own ships. Arron joined him there, a cup of hot coffee and a doughnut in hand.

"Here," Arron said, shoving the coffee and doughnut at Spraker. "I can't remember the last time you stopped for something to eat. You're going to need all the energy you can get."

"Thanks, Mom," Spraker shot Arron a wry look as he took the coffee and bit into the doughnut.

"Frankly, sir," Arron said in all seriousness, "you're the best hope any of us has right now making it home alive and it's my job to make sure you can do yours properly."

"Have I said I miss my wife recently?" Spraker mumbled around his mouthful of doughnut.

"Not in the last few minutes, sir, but I understand how you feel."

Spraker swallowed and took a sip of his coffee. "I want the *Peart*'s CIWS programmed to open fire on the squids as soon as they're detected. Our best bet is going to be keeping them off this ship entirely. Even with the precautions we're all taking, if they get onto the decks, I don't know that we'll be able to stop them."

"Already done so, sir," Arron said, grinning.

"And make sure we keep trying to contact the other ships of the DESRON. I know it's unlikely, but I am holding out hope that three frigates here aren't the only survivors. I'll be in my quarters if you need me."

****

It had taken half an hour to get back onboard the *Rogue*. Cordova didn't mind the time. The navy was very much about the concept of hurry up and wait. What he did mind was how Spraker had treated him. They had known each for a long time and all of a sudden Spraker was acting like he was suddenly so superior. He wouldn't have guessed that rank, certainly not a mere acting one, would go to Spraker's head so quickly. Cordova knew Spraker well enough to know from how he had acted, Spraker had come close to relieving him of command, maybe even having thrown into the brig. Well, Spraker could go frag himself. His plan was crap. And all that junk about the squids was crap too. There was no way on God's blue Earth that a shoal of squids, mutated or not, was the level of threat Spraker was acting like it was. If something had happened to the main body of DESRON 22, it was because Surface Community Captain Marcus was an idiot. How the man had ever gotten his rank was beyond Cordova's understanding. He knew Spraker felt the same about him and Cordova couldn't blame him for it. Marcus was a pencil pusher and a desk jockey at best. He didn't understand what real service was like. The fact that he was a coward in Cordova's opinion only added to the level of damage someone like Marcus could do with the rank he held.

Cordova passed on Spraker's orders to his crew and they set about welding the exterior doors closed and all that other rubbish. Whether it would help or not if the squids got onboard the *Rogue,* Cordova didn't care. He had no intentions of the letting the shoal anywhere near his ship. That wasn't how the navy was supposed to fight. The *Rogue* had torpedoes and deck guns for a reason and he planned to use them against the squids as soon as the creatures gave him the chance.

Spraker could talk a good game, sure. He knew, too, that Spraker wasn't a coward even if he was acting like one now. Cordova shook his head and wondered had happened to the Spraker he knew. This new one sucked hardcore. He half expected Spraker to come aboard the *Rogue* to make sure the orders he had given had been carried out.

"That bad, huh?" Selena asked as she entered Cordova's office and saw not only the expression he wore but the open bottle of Rum on his desk.

"That bad," he confirmed. "Spraker's a jerk now like the rest of the brass."

"I thought the two of you were close," Selena said as she moved to take a seat on the edge of Cordova's desk. Any other CO would've busted her for such behavior but not him. The two of them had shared more than a few inappropriately intimate meetings. Cordova wondered if her knees had healed up from the last one but decided now wasn't the time to check up on them with Spraker breathing down his neck.

"So did I," Cordova laughed, it was a cold and dark laugh full of sadness and resignation to a bitter truth.

"The stories about the killer squids are true then?"

"Apparently," Cordova sighed. "I'll believe it when see them, though."

He noticed Selena was staring at him and added, "I mean, there's something out there for sure. Don't get me wrong, I just don't think whatever it is, squids or not, is as bad as Spraker is letting that it is."

"Does he have a plan for getting us all out of here alive beyond the stuff you have the rest of the crew working on?"

"No," Cordova admitted. "He didn't. If we're going to make it through this, we're going to have make it on our own in spite of Spraker."

"I can hear in your voice, Cordova," Selena purred. "You have a plan of your own, don't you?"

Cordova smiled. "Don't I always?"

"And just how illegal is it?" Selena laughed.

"Spraker's not going to like it." Cordova joined in her laughter. "He's not going to like it all."

****

Lex stopped the crewman who was rushing passed him in the corridor. The crewman shook loose of his grasp but paused long enough to see what Lex needed him for.

"Where's Commander Spraker?" Lex demanded to know.

"He's on the bridge, Mr. Iver, getting the *Peart* and the other two frigates accompanying us underway."

The crewman raced away, leaving Lex standing alone in the corridor. He watched the man go. Lex wasn't even sure what he was doing in trying to find Commander Spraker. He'd told him already about his theory on the squids. He wasn't so sure that Spraker had really understood him, though. If what Les was thinking was right, he needed Spraker to understand it clearly or they might all pay the price for it.

Lex headed for the *Peart*'s bridge. It was two decks up from where he currently was and he took the long way around to reach it hoping that the walk would give him time to get his own thoughts in order. Lex knew that Spraker wasn't going to want to listen. Though Spraker no longer wrote him off as utterly insane and had even humbled himself to the point of coming back for a second visit with him to get advice on the monsters, Lex was sure that Spraker didn't like him. Where that dislike originated from, who knew? And did even matter? They didn't have to like each other in order to work together to get everyone out of this mess, but Lex was just a civilian. He couldn't really do anything. He could only influence, he hoped, those who could.

As Lex reached the bridge, he found its entrance blocked by two armed guards. He recognized both of them. They had been part of the boarding parties that stormed the *Pleasure Bound* and saved his life. If he remembered correctly, the little guy was named Fox and the woman, Diana.

"Can I help you, Mr. Iver?" Diana asked.

"I need to see Commander Spraker," Lex told her, trying his best to edge by her. Diana moved to block his path.

"Sorry, man," Fox said. "The commander has a lot going on right now."

"It's urgent," Lex pleaded.

Diana and Fox exchanged a look but neither of them moved aside.

"Tell you what, buddy," Fox nodded at him with a sly smile. "We'll let the commander know you're here. I can't promise he'll see you, but it's the best we can do. Cool?"

"Sure," Lex agreed, not seeing that he had any other option. He certainly couldn't shove his way past two heavily armed marines. On a good day, he figured he might could have taken Fox if luck was on his side, but that Diana...with her, he didn't stand a chance. Ever.

****

Spraker sat in his command chair. The trio of frigates was underway with the *Peart* in the lead. Spraker was making sure they kept their speed at normal levels despite that every nerve in his body longed to give the order to push their engines to the breaking point. He had no desire to enter an engagement with the squids. Knowing they had apparently taken out a quartet of destroyers and not having any details on the squids' numbers or remaining strength, doing so was just too dangerous. Cordova had made the argument that the creatures were just animals and that a coordinated attack could prevail against them, but Spraker just wasn't willing to gamble with the lives of those of DESRON 22 who were still alive.

Arron stood beside him, looking as nervous as Spraker felt. It was odd to see Arron on edge. His XO was one of the most level-headed officers Spraker had ever known. If Arron was creeped out, that meant things were really bad.

So far, there had been no sign of the squids. Luke sat hunched over the sonar station, running sweep after sweep, as he kept an eye out for the things. Megan worked frantically at the communications station, still trying to get the long-range comm. back online. From the nasty expression she wore, Spraker could tell she wasn't having any luck at it. Whatever was causing the strange interference remained a mystery. The ship's own systems were fine according to Megan. Beyond that, there was nothing else she could tell him.

Luke suddenly sat up straight as if a jolt of electric shock had run through his body. His eyes were wide as he called out, "Commander Spraker! I am picking up numerous contacts, subsurface and closing fast."

"It's them," Arron whispered behind him, barely loud enough for Spraker to hear.

"E.T.A.?" Spraker asked, shifting in his chair to look at Luke.

"E.T.A. in ten, sir. They're still a long way out," Luke told him.

"Good work," Spraker smiled at the sonar officer. "Have the fleet increase speed to maximum. Give us everything she's got," he added to his own helmsman.

"Are you sure that's a good idea?" Arron cautioned.

"They know we're here, Arron, and they're coming whether we run or not at this point," Spraker pointed out. "We may as well make them work for it."

Arron grunted in agreement but stayed silent otherwise.

"The squids are increasing speed to match!" Luke reported.

The next two minutes ticked by like hours as the squids continued to close on the formation of frigates.

"If you're hoping they'll give up and break off, I think you're out of luck, sir," Arron commented.

Spraker glared at him. He was right but that didn't make the news any easier to hear.

"Sir!" Luke interrupted. "The *Rogue!* She's changed course, sir."

"What?" Spraker raged, nearly leaping from his chair. "What the blazes does Cordova think he's doing?"

"I don't know, but he's changed his heading towards the squids!" Luke reported.

Megan interrupted Luke and Spraker. "Commander Mills is requesting to speak with you, sir!"

"Put him on," Spraker ordered her.

"Spraker, Cordova's changed his course to engage the shoal of squids. Do we follow?" Mills asked, the confusion and fear in his voice clear.

"No," Spraker slammed a clenched fist into the arm of his chair. "That idiot is going to get himself killed. Maintain your original course and speed, Commander Mills. That's an order."

****

Cordova grinned like a madman as he stood on the bridge of the *Rogue* staring out the ship's forward window, his hands locked behind his back. His crew was in full support of his plan. If there were those onboard who weren't, they were keeping their mouths shut about it.

Selena stood beside him. Her blue eyes were filled with a deadly eagerness. If anyone backed him on this, it was her. He had briefed the crew of the *Rogue* extensively on his plan. It was simple. If the chance arose, he hoped to engage the squids at a distance and use the *Rogue*'s long-range weapons, including her newly hull-mounted torpedo launchers to take the squids under guns at good distance out and blow the creatures to pieces before they ever reached what was left of DESRON 22.

His gunnery officer, Len, was already acquiring his targets when Cordova gave the order, "Len, give 'em Hell."

"Yes, sir," Len answered, smiling back at Cordova.

Len emptied everything that the *Rogue* had at the squids in one massive barrage. Deck cannons boomed as torpedoes splashed into the water from her twin front-mounted tubes to go streaking at their target.

"Direct hit!" Len informed him.

Cordova watched the distant impact through a pair of binoculars through the *Rogue*'s forward window. Geysers of erupted from the ocean's previously calm surface as massive shells splashed down upon the shoal of squids. The waters were already thickened by the blackness of the squids' blood as the torpedoes reached them only moments later. A second round of explosions detonated beneath the waves.

Gary, the *Rogue*'s on-duty sonar tech yelled out, "The shoal's main body is breaking up, sir! It looks like some of the squids are trying to alter their course and run."

"Some?" Cordova barked. "I need more than that."

"The bulk of the shoal is still on course for us, sir," Gary replied. "The shoal has taken a lot of damage though. At best guess, I'd say the shoal has lost around fifteen percent of its density."

"Gary, if you would." Cordova waved at the gunnery officer.

"With pleasure, sir." Len showed his teeth as his fingers danced over the controls of the weapons' station and loosed two more waves of death at the squids.

"The squids are taking evasive maneuvers this time, sir!" Gary yelled.

Cordova continued to keep an eye on the water through his binoculars.

The second volley from the *Rogue* struck the squids. It wasn't as devastating as the first, but it still did a great deal of damage from the looks of things. The third followed closely on its heels. By now, a massive swathe of the ocean, in front of the *Rogue,* had become a churning sea of blackness.

"Sir!" Gary shouted excitedly. "The *Drake* has come about to join us. She's just opened fire on the shoal of squids herself!"

"I'll be da—" Cordova started but Selena cut in over top of him.

"I am really starting to believe this plan of yours is going to work, Commander Cordova," Selena purred, drawing closer to him. Inappropriately close, but Cordova didn't care. He was too busy savoring his victory to even notice.

"Between the fire from the *Drake* and our own, the shoal's density is down by over fifty percent sir!" Gary was beaming as if Cordova's plan had been his own.

Selena pulled away from Cordova as the comm. officer waved her over. Selena bent and spoke with the officer hurriedly. When she was done, she walked back towards where Cordova stood.

"Commander, Spraker is on the priority channel for you," she chuckled. "He's rather a bit upset it seems."

"I bet so," Cordova laughed loudly. "I bet he's wishing he had the balls to try what we just did."

"You know he's going to court martial you." Selena placed a hand on his shoulder.

"Let him try," Cordova urged. "I think the results of my actions speak rather loudly for themselves, don't you?"

Selena cocked her head with a wry grin. "Results are what matter the most to command."

The *Rogue* and the *Drake* had continued firing on the shoal. Len had just launched the *Rogue*'s sixth volley when Gary motioned for Cordova's attention.

Cordova was still watching the distant carnage through his binoculars. Selena nudged him and pointed at Gary. Cordova let his binoculars dangle on the cord that bound them to his neck as he left his ship's window and moved towards its sonar station.

"Sir, I'd estimate the squids have taken more than sixty percent losses. They've broken off their course towards the fleet and are scattering randomly in the water," Gary told him. Cordova sensed a but coming though.

"Good." Cordova squeezed Gary's shoulder with his right hand.

"But there's something else out there, sir," Gary tapped the sonar screen with his pointer finger.

Cordova leaned forward to glance at the screen over Gary's shoulder. His eyes bugged as he saw the size of the image on the screen. "What in the devil is that? It's big enough to be a freaking island."

Gary could only shake his head. "I don't know, sir, but whatever it is, it appears to have been hiding behind the shoal of squids or within it. Now that the squids have dispersed, it's picking up speed towards us."

"Len?" Cordova called.

"Already taking it with guns, sir. It's so massive I don't think I even need a firm lock to hit it."

"Then do so," Cordova snapped.

The triumphant atmosphere of the *Rogue*'s bridge quickly became one of fear and dread.

****

Spraker was cursing like the veteran sailor he was as he watched the *Rogue* and the *Drake* engaging the squids. He couldn't believe Mills had turned on him to support Cordova. He would've thought Mills had more sense than that. Spraker couldn't argue with the results the two ships had achieved, though. Under their combined fire, the squids had been broken and driven off. He mind was reeling, trying to come up with a way to handle the situation with Cordova and Mills' blatant disregard for his orders when it appeared the action they had taken had been the correct one.

"This is bad," Arron commented.

"Tell me about it," Spraker raged.

"No, sir," Arron shot him a look from where he stood at the sonar station. "I don't mean the mess with those two idiots. I mean what's out there in the water."

Spraker whirled on him, terrified he already knew what Arron was about to tell him.

"It looks like Iver's theories on the squids were right again, sir," Arron frowned.

"You don't mean…"

"Yes, sir," Arron said. "The *mom* has just shown herself."

Spraker raced over to the sonar station to take a look at the screen for himself. What he saw sent shivers of cold fear running along his spine.

"How big is that thing?" Spraker muttered more to himself than anyone in particular.

Arron shrugged. "Hard to get an accurate reading sir. A hell of a lot bigger than us, though. That thing looks like it could go head to head with a battleship and still have the odds be in its favor."

"Is it coming after us?" Spraker asked. The *Peart* had maintained her course and speed away from the shoal of squids while the *Rogue* and the *Drake* had engaged it.

"No, sir," Arron said, "She's on a direct course for Cordova and Mills' ships. And pouring on the speed too. She's pushing thirty-five knots at the moment and climbing."

"Dear God," Spraker stammered. With speed like that, not even the *Peart*'s head start would matter if she decided to come after them. She'd overtake them in less than a half hour, maybe a lot less.

"The *Rogue* and the *Drake* are opening fire on her," Arron reported. "Should we come about to join them?"

Spraker wasn't the sort of commander who hesitated in the decisions he made but this time he did. He just didn't have an answer. If he ordered the *Peart* to come around and join the other two ships maybe, just maybe, they could stop that thing out there with their combined firepower. If they failed to do so though, all three ships would certainly be lost. His gut told him that the mother squid wasn't going to give up as easily as her children had. If he engaged her, it would be a fight to the death with the deck stacked in her favor. She didn't even need to destroy the three frigates. If she managed to just hurt them badly then her children could come back screeching down on the damaged vessels to finish them.

As he rolled over what to do in his mind, his thoughts went to Captain Wirtz. He wished the grizzled, old veteran were here. Wirtz would know what to do if anyone did. It was too bad the old man was likely dead.

"Commander?" Arron urged him. "Your orders?"

"Keep our course steady," Spraker ordered at last. "I just don't think we can take that thing out there. Not even with all three ships acting together."

"I agree, sir," Arron assured him. "Besides, someone has to make it out of here alive to let the brass back home know what's happened here."

****

Commander Mills of the *Drake* was quickly beginning to regret his choice to support the *Rogue* in her engagement of the shoal of squids as he watched the massive, almost mountain-sized *thing* in the water closing on his vessel. During the engagement, the *Drake* had slipped passed the *Rogue*'s forward position and now was not only directly in that monster's path but was the closest ship to it as well.

Never in his life had Mills dreamed things like the monster out there could exist in the real world. They were supposed to only exist in the minds of madmen and in horror films. Yet, that thing was out there and coming straight for him.

"Take that monster with guns and fire at will!" he screamed.

Torpedoes streaked from the *Drake's* hull-mounted launchers toward the approaching abomination.

"Contact!" his weapons officer reported. "Direct hit, all rounds!"

Mills had never taken his eyes away from the approaching beast. The rounds may have struck it but if so, they didn't even slow it down.

He opened his mouth to give another order but never got the chance. The mega-squid reached the *Drake.* The monster hit the frigate with such force that the *Drake* rolled in the water. Mills heard the whine of metal being bent inward and torn apart as the deck shifted beneath him and he lost his footing. He tumbled to land awkwardly on his shoulder with the cracking sound bones breaking. His face twisted into a grimace of pain as a muffled grunt escaped his lips.

All around him, his crew was panicking. Stations blew out, erupting in showers of sparks and flames. The forward window of the bridge shattered, sending pieces of jagged glass flying like shrapnel. He watched his helmsman take a shard of glass to his throat and collapse, bleeding out in fast flowing streams of red onto the ship's controls. The men and women of the bridge crew were screaming. Some of them shouted pleas to God for mercy while other loosed litanies of curses and other still merely howled like animals driven mad by fear.

Mills tried to get back to his feet, but the pain of the attempt was too much for him. He could taste blood on his tongue and knew his fall had hurt him far worse than just his broken shoulder joint. He wanted to shout out the order to abandon ship but all he could do was grit his teeth and try to stay conscious.

The *Drake* righted itself on the waves for a moment until something else seemed to strike the entire ship at once. In Mills' mind, he envisioned the tentacles of the giant monster wrapping around the ship's hull. The next thing he knew, there was water rushing onto the bridge through the busted forward window and he knew, just knew, the mother squid was taking the *Drake* under the waves with her.

The wave of rushing water picked Mills up from where he lay on the deck as it engulfed him. The saltwater stung his wide, bugged-out eyes as he opened his mouth to scream and the water entered his lungs.

****

Cordova watched the destruction of the *Drake* like a nightmare unfolding before his very eyes. One minute, the *Drake* had been between the *Rogue* and the massive, enraged mother squid, the next she was simply gone. It all had happened so fast. The mega-squid had rammed into the *Drake,* collapsing a good portion of her hull and causing the *Drake* to almost capsize in the water. Then, in an instant, the mega-squid had wrapped its insanely long tentacles around the *Drake* dragged her beneath the waves.

"Get us the Hell out of here!" Cordova barked at the *Rogue*'s helmsman. "Maximum power! Burn the blasted engine up if you have to!"

"Yes, sir!" the helmsman shouted, not needing to be told twice.

Selena had gone pale as a ghost beside Cordova. She reached for him but he shoved her away.

"Mind your place, woman," he spat at her.

Cordova saw anger flare in Selena's eyes, but he had far bigger things to deal with and utterly didn't give a crap.

"Is that thing coming after us?" Cordova yelled at his sonar tech even as he ran towards the station to check for himself.

"No, sir! It's still pulling the *Drake* down."

"Good," Cordova hoped the monster would take its time with the *Drake*. Every minute it spent delivering its vengeance to the *Drake* beneath the waves was that much more time his own ship had to pull away.

"Where's the *Peart?*" Cordova demanded to know.

Selena had joined him at the sonar station, though she did her best to stay out of his reach or perhaps keep him out of hers. "Spraker never changed course. He's got at least a good ten minutes head start on us. Even at our top speed, we'll never overtake him unless he slows down."

"That coward isn't going to slow down." Cordova clenched his fists. "He's going to keep right on running like what he's done so far and that means we're next on the list of that thing's targets when it's done with the *Drake.*"

"We can't outrun it," Selena told him. "It was pushing forty knots when it rammed Mills' ship."

Cordova had never felt so helpless and it only made severed to make him angrier. He couldn't run and fighting seemed like suicide.

"You got a plan for this?" Selena mocked him, her lips pulled back into a sneer.

"Sir!" his sonar tech shouted. "The mega-squid has released the *Drake* and is on her way back up to the surface!"

"Where will she emerge?" Cordova asked, planning to have her taken with guns and at least get in a parting shot at the beast before it finished the *Rogue* and him along with her.

The sonar tech's reply sounded like the screech of little girl as he answered, "Directly beneath us, sir!"

There was no time for anything else. The mega-squid thudded into the *Rogue*'s underside with such force that she rose up from the water into the air. Her hull ruptured in numerous places even before the mega-squid's tentacles lashed out to embrace her. The tentacles squeezed tighter and tighter as metal fractured and bent. Somewhere, in the bowels of the *Rogue,* the jagged pieces of a folding inward wall put too much pressure on a container of ordnance for her aft torpedo launchers. The crewmen in that area of the ship died instantly as flames washed over them and an explosion shook the *Rogue*'s already-broken form. It triggered a series of secondary explosions that ran the length of the ship. One boom of fire and flying bits of hull after another rang out until the entire ship blossomed into a bright, blinding burst of fire.

The mother squid shrieked as her prey unexpectedly exploded in her grasp. She released the blazing remnants of the *Rogue* and speed away from them, leaving a trail of black blood in her wake.

****

Everyone on the bridge of the *Peart* heard the explosion that ripped the *Rogue* apart over the open squadron channel. The *Rogue*'s comm. officer had been broadcasting over the DESRON's primary channeling, shouting out a desperate plea for help up until the moment the *Rogue* was no more.

Spraker felt a pang of guilt. Cordova had been his friend no matter how much of a jerk the guy was. Spraker knew he had done all he could to keep Cordova in line, but it hadn't been enough and he wondered if just maybe he could have done something more. Maybe he should have tossed Cordova in the brig and replaced him as commander of the *Rogue*. It didn't matter now, though. Cordova was gone and the entire crew of the *Rogue* with him. Not a single lift boat had hit the water. The explosion had just happened too fast and without any warning.

Mills and his ship, the *Drake*, were gone too, having followed Cordova into a battle that never should have taken place. Spraker still couldn't figure why Mills had done it. Sure, Cordova had appeared to be beating back the squids but Spraker's orders to avoid engagement of the creatures had also been very clear. Now, there was only the *Peart* left. One frigate was all that remained from what once had been a full-strength DESRON including four destroyers and their support vessels.

No matter what Spraker did, he was fairly sure he was going to be brought up on charges when he got home, *if* he and his crew got home. The brass back home were going to need someone to blame and he was the only commanding officer left. The loss of so many ships wasn't something that could just be overlooked or swept under the rug. Oh, he was sure the brass would try to do just that. They wouldn't want to the public to know about the existence of the squids much less that the creatures had engaged DESRON 22 and beaten it. The existence of the squids would cause worldwide panic among mariners if word about it got out and the loss of the DESRON would be taken as a sign of weakness by the enemies of the United States. If a squids could defeat the United States on the open waters, the United States' enemies would surely feel they could too.

Cordova may have been a fool, but his death hadn't been in vain. The man had beaten back the main body of the smaller squids and the explosion of the *Rogue,* while in the mega-squid's grasp, had appeared to injure it. The massive monster had fled the burning wreckage of the *Rogue* at a speed well over thirty knots, leaving a trail of its thick, black blood in the water behind it. Spraker didn't dare hope the thing's injury was enough to keep it from circling around to engage the *Peart,* though. Nonetheless, Cordova and the crew of the *Rogue* had bought him time.

Spraker had the *Peart* running full out now, her engines straining to muster all the speed that could be forced out of them. He knew it wouldn't be enough. The best he could hope for was to gain a few more minutes of safety before the mother squid shook off her pain and came after them. There was a risk the *Peart*'s engines would fail being pushed as hard as they were, but Spraker saw the risk as worth it. Every second he could buy his ship and crew mattered. Each one gave them that much longer to come up a plan on how to deal with the mother squid. The problem was that Spraker wasn't sure there was a way to deal with the thing. She was so massive that the odds of killing her with the weapons he had at hand were slim unless he used the *Peart* itself as a bomb just as Cordova had unintentionally done with his ship the *Rogue.* Spraker had to admit to his self that he might have considered doing just that and having his crew abandon ship beforehand if it wasn't for the fact that the smaller squids weren't entirely beaten. There were enough of the small creatures out there to make short work of any lifeboats that he put into the water. The life boats only defense would be the small arms of their passengers and the small squids would easily overwhelm them through sheer numbers.

Spraker's dark musings were brought to an end as his XO, Arron, approached him.

"Sir, Mr. Iver is waiting on you just outside of the bridge. He's requested to speak with you."

Shrugging, Spraker rose from his command chair. "Sure, why not? Time is all we have left at this point and there's nothing we can do until that thing out there decides to make its move."

****

Lex Iver desperately longed for a cigarette as he stood outside the entrance to the *Peart*'s bridge waiting on Commander Sparker to agree to see him. If the two marines, Diana and Fox, who stood guard, blocking his path, were to be believed, they had let Spraker know he was there. Lex had, for the most part, quit smoking years ago. Mary had made him promise to give it up when they got married. Even so, it took all his willpower not to ask one of the marines if they had a smoke.

He noticed Diana cock her head and place a finger on the earpiece that was part of her combat helmet.

"Mr. Iver," she told him, "the commander has agreed to see you, sir."

"Thank you," Lex told the two marines as they moved out of his path to allow him to enter the bridge.

The ship's XO, Arron, met Lex as he entered the bridge. Arron greeted him with a weak attempt at a smile. "It's good to see you again, Mr. Iver."

"If by that you mean it's good we're all still alive, I wholeheartedly agree," Lex laughed. "Anything I need to be made of aware of before I see the commander?"

Arron paused before answering Lex's strange question. Lex Iver wasn't a part of the DESRON's chain of command or even part of the *Peart*'s crew. He was a civilian, horror author that they had rescued from the cruise liner, the *Pleasure Bound,* when all the madness they were now living in had begun. Still, Lex's insight on the squids had proved extremely valuable. Without it, they might all have been dead already.

"I'm not sure what you mean, sir," Arron answered cautiously.

"Cut the crap, Arron. Military protocols be damned. I have a right to know what's happening out there. I'm stuck on this frigate just as much as you are." Lex stood up tall as he demanded the information from Arron.

With a heavy sigh, Arron started talking. "We were engaged by the squids or rather the other two remaining frigates of the DESRON engaged them. Both of those frigates were lost but not before doing a great deal of damage to the lesser squids."

"Lesser squids?" Lex repeated the words even as he reeled from hearing that the *Peart* was now the only remaining vessel of DESRON 22. "I take it my theory that was a mother creature out there somewhere has proved true and you've seen her."

"Yes, sir," Arron nodded. "However, I think it best that Commander Spraker tell you anything else you wish to know. If you'll follow me, he's waiting for you in his ready room."

Lex followed the big executive officer to the door of Spraker's ready room and allowed Arron to open it for him. Arron gave him a parting look that that told him Spraker was just as worried about their current situation as he was.

Spraker sat behind his desk, puffing on a cigarette as he stared through the ready room's sole window at the waves beyond it. His gaze shifted to Lex as the horror author entered.

"I hear you need to see me," Spraker commented.

Lex nodded, eying the pack of smokes that laid on top of Spraker's desk. Spraker must have noticed.

"Go ahead and fire one up if you want," Spraker gestured at the pack and the lighter next to it. "It's likely to be your last one."

"Your XO just told me that this ship is the only left," Lex commented.

Spraker frowned. "You were right about the mother squid thing. She's massive like some sort of Kraken right out myth, only larger than I would ever have imagined could exist in the real world."

Lex took a cigarette from Spraker's pack and lit it. He drew a long drag of smoke into his lungs and savored the feeling of it before replying, "A Kraken. I suppose that's as good a name for that monster out there as any."

"What do you want, Mr. Iver?" Spraker said, getting down to business.

"I wanted to warn you about the Kraken," Lex chuckled darkly. "I guess I'm too late."

"You told me about the thing when we last talked, Mr. Iver. I just wasn't ready to hear you then. Oh, I listened I guess but I wasn't ready to believe it…and we've all paid the price for it too."

"So that's it then?" Lex challenged Spraker. "You're just giving up?"

"What else can I do, Mr. Iver?" Spraker took a final puff from his cigarette and ground out the glowing ember of its butt in the ashtray in front of him. "We can't outrun the thing. We can't seem to get a distress call out no matter what we do. And let me tell you, from what I have seen, we sure don't have the firepower to fight it."

Lex grunted. "I, for one, would like to do more than just sit here waiting on that monster to show up and have us for its next meal, Commander."

"Then I hope you have a plan, Mr. Iver, because I sure don't," Spraker admitted.

"I wrote some Kaiju books early in my career, Commander," Lex laughed. "The monsters always won in them."

"Arron mentioned that. My XO is rather a fan of your work."

Lex smiled. "Not that it matters. I won't be writing anything else unless we come up with some means of getting out here alive."

"Like I said, Mr. Iver, I'm fresh out of miracles." Spraker shook his head in frustration.

Lex and Spraker both flinched as the *Peart*'s CIWS sprang to life. The fire of the automated defense system sounded like a continuous roar of thunder. The *Peart*'s alarm klaxons began to blare as Spraker leaped from his seat, rushing towards the bridge with Lex following after him.

"I guess you're right, Iver," Spraker laughed. "It's just not in me to go down without a fight!"

****

Spraker nearly collided with Arron as he raced onto the bridge. The large XO was in a panic.

"She's back?" Spraker shouted. "The Kraken?"

Arron stared at his commander. "Kraken? Is that what we're calling that monster now?"

Spraker glared at Arron.

"No, sir!" Arron reported, snapping to attention, at the look of pure anger in Spraker's eyes. "It's the small squids, sir. They came out of nowhere! Somehow the sonar didn't detect them until they were right on top of us."

****

Robert Vancel was the ranking officer of the marines aboard the *Peart*. The command actually belonged to Page though. Vancel's was only supposed to be on the ship as an observer during DESRON 22's shakedown maneuvers. Given the direness of the mess they were in though, Vancel had taken command. He and Page stood together on the *Peart*'s forward deck, accompanied by over half of the frigates marines, watching the squids come. The darted through the water like red blurs of lightning. The ship's CIWS was letting the creatures have it too. The virtual wall of bullets it pumped into the water as the squids closed in caused to it churn and grow black. Vancel couldn't even guess at how many squids were being ripped apart beneath the waves. The number had to be staggering. Yet, the creatures came on. Those who made it passed the fire of the CIWS leaped from the waves onto the *Peart*'s hull. Each of them clinging to the spot where the landed just long enough to orientate themselves. Then, they began their climb. Vancel watched a squid flinging one of its tentacled clubs upwards to pierce the metal of the side of the ship. It used that tentacle to heave its body up, rolling over itself as it went, to lash out its other tentacled club and hook into the ship even higher. The process was carried out with a speed almost equal to that the squids demonstrated in the water. Hundreds of the creatures swarmed the *Peart* in such a manner, despite the fire of the CIWS.

"You ready for this?" Vancel asked Page as he chambered a round in his shotgun.

Page gave Vancel a quick nod, readying his M-16. "It's what we get paid for, sir."

The two of them backed away from the edge of the deck to allow the squids to come over it without resistance. Vancel wanted the creatures to pile into the large, open kill zone of the forward deck and they obliged him.

Vancel and the *Peart*'s marines concentrated their fire at the largest cluster of the monsters in the bow of the ship. One squid took a round from Vancel shotgun and blew apart in a spray of black blood and jagged pieces of torn meat. Page poured his fire into another of the creatures. Its body jerked as burst after burst from Page's M-16 ripped into it. Someone tossed a grenade over Vancel and Page. It landed into a group of squids who had gathered near the forward railing. The explosion hurt Vancel's ears as the squids caught in its blast were all but disintegrated from the shrapnel that was sent flying out in all directions.

The marines didn't let up, but even so, the squids were gaining ground. For each one that fell, another made it that much closer to the marines' position. The mass of the squids continued to press forward in such a manner until a .50 cal, located on the command deck of the *Peart*, overlooking the battle, began to chatter. Its high-powered stream of fire swept over the squids like a scythe raking down rows of wheat. A cheer went up from the ship's defenders as they continued their fight.

Vancel looked towards the .50 cal emplacement to see that Page's "men," Diana and Fox, were responsible for bringing the heavy weapon to their aid. He thanked God for them as Diana clutched the weapon's firing mechanism, mowing down the squids in her line of fire, and Fox did his best to keep the ammo flowing to her.

"We have to hold them here!" Vancel shouted, trying to make his voice heard over the cacophony around him.

"Sir!" he heard Page scream at him. Even so, Vancel didn't see the squid that was flinging itself at him until it was too late. The squid landed on him, its arms wrapping around his upper body. Vancel's shotgun clattered to the deck at his feet as the creature's limbs tightened. Vancel looked down at the thing just in time to see its beak-like mouth dig into his guts. He screamed as the squid's mouth worked. It reached inside him through the open wound that was now the bulk of his stomach pulling out strands of red-slicked intestines. Vancel's arms were caught and jerked outwards from his body the squid's tentacles, exposing even more of his body to the reach of the thing's beck. As Vancel's resistance grew weaker, the squid lowered some of its own legs to support the weight of the two of them and keep Vancel on his feet as it continued to feast on him.

Page's mouth filled with vomit as he watched what was happening to Vancel. He spat it out and took aim at his CO's head. A three-round burst from his rifle put Vancel out of his misery, splattering the older man's brain matter into the air as they blew apart his skull. Only then did Page turn his attention to the squid holding up Vancel's corpse as its beak continued to strike out at it, tearing away rib bones and strips of exposed lung tissue. Page put a burst into the squid's side. The creature screeched as it released Vancel's corpse and tried to flee. Page's second burst finished the monster as its bullets produced large holes in its main body. The squid flopped to the deck, leaking black blood that pooled quickly around its motionless form.

Sensing movement in the air to his left, Page ducked just in time to escape a squid landing on him. The creature flew over him and landed roughly on the deck. It lashed out with one of its limbs, slashing a deep, red groove of torn flesh along Page's inner right thigh. Page clenched his teeth against the pain as he rammed the barrel of his weapon *into* the squid's main body mass before squeezing its trigger. An explosion of splattering black blood rained over him. The squid's blood was cold and slime-like against his exposed skin. There was no time to wipe it off, though. The .50 cal on the deck above the battle had fallen silent and the squids were pressing forward with renewed fury.

"Fall back!" Page yelled at the top of his lungs before he realized that most, if not all, of his men were already dead. He stood alone, surrounded by hungry, madden monsters from the depths of the ocean.

"Oh, crap," were Page's last words before dozens and dozens of tentacles lashed out to grab his arms, legs, throat, and torso. The ends of others buried themselves in his eye sockets. Still others dug into his stomach and wriggled through his innards. One even inverted his genitals as it rammed upwards between his legs into his body.

The deck of the *Peart* was slick with the blood of both men and squid as the creatures finished Page and began to make their way towards the welded-shut entrances that led into the ship's interior.

****

Diana and Fox had abandoned the .50 cal on the command deck as they neared the end of the weapon's ready ammo. Diana hated doing so. They were basically leaving the rest of the marines engaged with the squids on the forward deck to die. Without the support of the .50, it would happen quickly too. Fox had an idea of how the rid the deck completely of the squids though and if his idea had even a remote shot of doing the job, it was something that had to try.

The two of them returned, carrying a large cylinder between them. They didn't even have to reach the railing and look down onto the forward deck for Diana to know that the others of their unit were dead.

"Come on!" Fox yelled at her, urging into action. The two of them flung the cylinder over the railing onto the deck below. There were squids everywhere below their position. Some of the creatures were even already making their way towards the wall to climb up it.

"You sure this is going to work?" Diana shouted over the hissing cries of the frenzied squids.

"It worked in my favorite zombie movie!" Fox assured her. "Just trust me on this, okay? Pop that sucker with your rifle and let's get this over with!"

Diana shouldered her M-16 and took aim at the cylinder on the lower deck. Ninety percent or more of the squids were still in that area. Vancel, Page, and the others had held them just long enough *if* Fox's insane plan actually worked. Diana released the air from her lungs slowly and centered her entire being on hitting her target. It wasn't going to be an easy shot as the cylinder was inside the mass of the squids that were swarming the *Peart*'s forward deck, but she figured she could make it if she just took her time and blocked out the chaos around her.

Her finger slid the trigger of her M-16 back. The rifle jerked in her hands as a three-round burst sprayed from its barrel. The rounds struck true. They slammed into the cylinder of propane and then the world below her went white.

The explosion from the rupturing propane tank blossomed into an ever-growing ball of flame that swept across the entire forward deck. It stretched upwards towards the clouds as well, sending a wave of fire running up the wall directly at Diana's position. She threw herself back out of the fire's reach.

Diana felt Fox's hands on her shoulders, shaking her awake. He was smiling like an adrenaline junkie who had just gotten the fix of his life.

"Did it work?" Diana asked, rubbing at the growing bump on her forehead from where it had smacked the deck she had been standing on.

"Oh yeah, it worked," Fox laughed. "Those fraggers got fired big time!"

Fox helped Diana to her feet. She looked over the scorched railing towards the forward deck. It was clear of live squids. Only smoking corpses littered it now…and a bloody lot of them too.

"How long have I been out?" Diana asked, jerking Fox closer to her by the front of his uniform.

"Not even a minute," he told her. "The best is that I think that blast got the message across to the rest of their shoal too. I haven't seen any more them trying to get onboard since the blast."

Diana allowed herself a smile as she stood there with Fox helping support her weight. It quickly turned to an expression stark terror as her eyes fell on the distant horizon. Fox must have seen it too because she heard him mumble, "What now?"

There in the distance, the mother squid rose from the depths to cruise along the surface of the ocean like an inbound torpedo, cutting a path of churning water straight towards the *Peart.*

****

Commander Spraker, his XO Arron, and Lex Iver had watched the battle taking place on the main deck of the *Peart.* Doing so had not been an easy thing for any of them. All of them breathed a sigh of relief when the battle had been won. It had been a costly thing. Reports were coming in that both of the marines' COs had perished in the battle. The ranking officer was now a lieutenant by the name of Diana. There were still a few scattered squids here and there aboard the *Peart,* but they were nothing that the remaining Security Alert teams couldn't handle. It was pretty much a mop-up operation at this point.

While Spraker was thankful to God that the marines had pulled off a miracle in driving the lesser squids away from the *Peart,* the ship was far from out of trouble. The mother squid, or Kraken as Spraker had begun calling it, was still out. The destruction of the *Rogue* had hurt her badly, but Spraker couldn't allow himself to believe it was enough to drive her away as well. No, she would be back. He could feel it.

"Helm, resume course. Maximum speed," Spraker ordered then turned to Megan. "Any luck breaking through the mysterious interference?"

"None, sir," Megan reported. "I'm sorry. I'm doing all I can, but whatever is blocking the long range comm. system is beyond me."

"Understood," Spraker nodded. "Keep at it anyway."

"Yes, sir." Megan returned to her work with a renewed determination.

"That..." Arron pointed at the deck outside the bridge window that was littered with the smoking corpses of squids, "that was a freaking miracle."

"Yeah," Lex agreed. "Let's just hope we didn't use up all our luck with it. We're going to need a lot more to escape the mother squid if she shows herself again."

"She will," Spraker told them both, leaving no room for argument.

****

The cleanup for the last squids aboard the *Peart* was completed in less than an hour with Diana and Fox leading the Security Alert teams to make sure it was done properly and there wouldn't be any nasty surprises waiting on them down the road. Spraker mourned the deaths of Vancel and Page. Both were veteran marines and the *Peart* would greatly feel their loss. For now, Lieutenant Diana had assumed command of both the ship's few remaining marines and its Security Alert teams. It had been the quick thinking of a marine named Fox that saved them all for the lesser squids' attack, yes, but he couldn't have pulled off his insane plan without Diana. The two of them both deserved commendations for their actions and Spraker vowed to see that they got them if the ship made it home.

Several hours had passed now since the squids attack and there was still no sign of the Kraken. Spraker knew the great beast was out there somewhere, biding its time and preparing for its own move against the *Peart*. Spraker kept the engineering staff of the *Peart* doing all they could to keep the ship's engines from burning out. The *Peart* had been pushing thirty knots ever since the attack on her had ended. He didn't dare risk reducing the ship's speed either. He knew, even with her head start, the Kraken could overtake her if the creature really wanted to. No, all he could do was get ready for the Kraken when it did choose to show itself.

The *Peart* was equipped with a MK-13 missile launcher that could send several volleys of harpoon anti-ship missiles into the water at long range, assuming they saw the Kraken's approach before it closed on the ship. The ship also had Mark 32 Anti-sub warfare tubes that could fire torpedoes in three-round barrages. The *Peart*'s last round of refits before she had left for this operation had doubled the number of those tubes she carried. She had two on her forward hull and two more aft. Spraker would have felt confident he could handle the Kraken, given the softer nature of such a creature's body, had it not been for the beast's size. It was going to take a heck of a lot of damage to take that thing out.

His XO, Arron, and Lex Iver were the bridge with him. Iver really had no place there in normal circumstances. The man wasn't military. He wasn't even a scientific expert on creatures like the Kraken. He was just a horror writer they had rescued from a cruise liner hit by the squids. That said, Iver's hunches and ability to think outside the box had kept them all alive more than once already. Spraker didn't like the man, but he knew a good resource when he saw it and Lex was that.

Lex had spent the hours since the attack helping Megan at the communications station. They still hadn't managed to come up with a means to cut through the interference that was keeping the long range comm. unusable but with Iver's help, Megan had determined its cause. The interference was a direct result of the large amount of bio-electrical energy the Kraken's insanely massive body generated. Knowing was half the battle, so Megan's efforts to crack through the interference at least had a direction now. The downside, though, was the strength of the interference confirmed that the Kraken was indeed somewhere close by, trailing the *Peart* as she tried to flee in the hope of reaching safer waters.

Luke yelled from the sonar station, his voice echoing across the enclosed space of the bridge. "Contact! It's the Kraken, sir!"

The crew was already at battle stations per Spraker's standing orders but nonetheless, alarm klaxons began to blare.

Arron had relieved the ship's weapons officer and taken command of that station himself. It was an unusual breach of SOPs, but Spraker had permitted it. He knew that Arron had worked his way up to XO from such positions and had seen Arron's talent with such systems keenly displayed over their years together.

"Bearing and speed?" Spraker snarled.

"She's coming in from the north, sir!" Luke answered. "Pushing thirty-five knots and still accelerating."

"She means to finish us," Lex told him. "And quickly. I'd wager she's done messing about after what happened to her with Cordova's ship."

"Understood," Spraker nodded at Lex then turned to address Arron. His XO was well ahead of him, though.

"Taking her with guns now, sir," Arron said. "Missiles away!"

The ship's MK-13 swiveled to acquire its target before Arron filled the sky with harpoons. The anti-ship missiles flew upwards before diving back down toward the water. The rained down on the approaching Kraken like arrows shot from Hell itself. The water's surface became a churning mass of black as waves splashed upwards toward the heavens.

"Direct hit!" Luke reported from the sonar station. "The Kraken is veering away, sir!"

"How bad is she hurt?" Spraker asked.

"Hard to say, sir," Luke frowned. "Her speed has dropped to roughly thirty knots, though, sir!"

"Hit her again," Spraker ordered Arron.

"I can't, sir," Arron informed him. "She's gone under. I can't get a good lock on her despite her size."

"She's off my screen," Luke cried out in panic. "I don't know if it's her depth or that blasted interference she's putting out but...she's gone."

Spraker clenched the arms of his command chair in rage and frustration.

"Could be she's running, sir," Arron offered, trying to stay positive.

"You and I both know that's the not the case, Arron," Spraker told his XO.

"Lex?" Spraker asked the horror writer. "Any ideas?"

Iver shook his head. "Not this time. Sorry."

"I've got her back on screen!" Luke screamed. "She's CBDR sir, coming up from beneath us!"

"Brace for impact!" Arron yelled before Spraker had the chance to himself.

The Kraken crashed into the underside of the *Peart,* its mass and velocity causing the frigate to rise up out of the water even as her hull crunched beneath the Kraken's fury. Metal ripped apart as it folded inwards.

The bridge crew was tossed about like ragdolls being slung around by an angry child. Lex went flying to slam into the comm. station where

Megan was strapped in. His neck snapped loudly from the impact. His head hung sideways at an unnatural angle where his corpse rested on the deck. Megan was screaming in outright terror, yet she made no move to unstrap herself from her station and try to help Iver. Spraker felt proud of her for that. She couldn't have done anything for the man anyway. He was already dead.

The ship was rocked about even harder as it splashed back onto the waves. Spraker was nearly flung from his command chair by the impact. Stations blew up into showers of sparks and fire all around the bridge. Whole sections of the ceiling gave away and tumbled down onto the bridge and its crew. One sailor was struck by a piece of the ceiling that swung downwards in an arc. It caught the man directly in the face, shattering his nose in a shower of blood. The man was flung backwards, off his feet, to go sliding across the bridge.

"We've got to..." Spraker heard Arron begin to yell but then the weapons station blew, taking him with it. Jagged bits of exploding metal and display screens tore through Arron's flesh like bullets, riddling the XO's body with gaping holes.

"No!" Spraker howled as he watched his longtime friend die.

All around the *Peart,* tentacles thicker than the trailers of eighteen wheelers rose from the waves to embrace her. They slapped into her with such force that her very hull fractured where metal met slimy flesh. Spraker felt the ship lurch and knew what was coming next. The Kraken was taking her down.

"Abandon ship!" he screamed at Megan, hoping she still had the means to pass on the order to the rest of the *Peart*'s crew. "All hands, abandon ship!"

Those words were Spraker's last as the forward window of the bridge shattered and sprayed the bridge and its crew with shards of glass that exploded inward like deadly missiles. Spraker took such a shard in the center of his throat. He felt the pain of the glass slicing completely through his neck for its tip to emerge from the backside of his neck and scrap against his command chair. Blood ran down the front of his uniform in rivers of red. He couldn't breathe or speak, but his mouth still worked, trying vainly to give orders.

Spraker's eyes bugged in his final moments as he watched the ocean come pouring in through the shattered forward window as the Kraken dragged the *Peart* downward into the depths with it.

EPILOGUE

Diana and Fox found themselves to be the only survivors of DESRON 22. The small life raft they shared bobbed about on the waves underneath the beautiful blue skies above. Fox had been badly injured during their flight for the raft and Diana had been forced to do the work of getting it functional and him onto it by herself. Fox lay unconscious, stretched out in the raft, his head resting in her lap. She could hear his soft moans of pain. Both of his legs were broken at the knees, badly. The white of bone protruded through both the red-soaked cloth of his pants and his flesh. Even if help arrived in time to save them, he'd never walk again. The damage done to his legs from his fall was just too much.

M-16 held ready, Diana watched the water around the raft. So far, there had been no sign of the lesser squids. There was no sign of the monstrously giant one either. She figured they were too small a target, for something like that thing to even notice. The lesser squids though…

Still, there was nothing she could but try to stay alert and wait. One way or another, they would be leaving these waters soon enough. It was just a question of who or what showed up hunting for them first. Someone would surely be coming to check on DESRON 22. An entire naval squadron didn't just disappear without someone back home asking why and sending help. Diana could only pray that help would arrive in time.

THE END

Eric S Brown is the author of numerous book series including the Bigfoot War series, the Kaiju Apocalypse series (with Jason Cordova), the Crypto-Squad series (with Jason Brannon), the Homeworld series (With Tony Faville and Jason Cordova), the Jack Bunny Bam series, and the A Pack of Wolves series. Some of his stand alone books include War of the Worlds plus Blood Guts and Zombies, World War of the Dead, Last Stand in a Dead Land, Sasquatch Lake, Kaiju Armageddon, Megalodon, Megalodons, and Megalodon Apocalypse to name only a few. His short fiction has been published hundreds of times in the small press and beyond including markets like the Onward Drake and Black Tide Rising anthologies from Baen Books, the Grantville Gazette, the SNAFU Military horror anthology series, and Walmart World magazine. He has done the novelizations for such films as Boggy Creek: The Legend is True (Studio 3 Entertainment) and The Bloody Rage of Bigfoot (Great Lake films). The first book of his Bigfoot War series was adapted into a feature by Origin Releasing in 2014. Werewolf Massacre at Hell's Gate was the second his books to be adapted into film in 2015. In addition to his fiction, Eric also writes an award winning comic book news column entitled "Comics in a Flash." Eric lives in North Carolina with his wife and two children where he continues to write tales of the hungry dead, blazing guns, and the things that lurk in the woods.

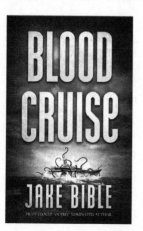

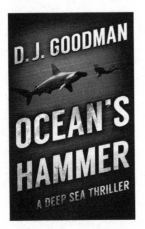

CHECK OUT OTHER GREAT
DEEP SEA THRILLERS

THEY RISE
by Hunter Shea

Some call them ghost sharks, the oldest and strangest looking creatures in the sea.

Marine biologist Brad Whitley has studied chimaera fish all his life. He thought he knew everything about them. He was wrong. Warming ocean temperatures free legions of prehistoric chimaera fish from their methane ice suspended animation. Now, in a corner of the Bermuda Triangle, the ocean waters run red. The 400 million year old massive killing machines know no mercy, destroying everything in their path. It will take Whitley, his climatologist ex-wife and the entire US Navy to stop them in the bloodiest battle ever seen on the high seas.

SERPENTINE
by Barry Napier

Clarkton Lake is a picturesque vacation spot located in rural Virginia, great for fishing, skiing, and wasting summer days away.

But this summer, something is different. When butchered bodies are discovered in the water and along the muddy banks of Clarkton Lake, what starts out as a typical summer on the lake quickly turns into a nightmare.

This summer, something new lives in the lake...something that was born in the darkest depths of the ocean and accidentally brought to these typically peaceful waters.

It's getting bigger, it's getting smarter...and it's always hungry.

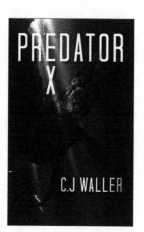

CHECK OUT OTHER GREAT DEEP SEA THRILLERS

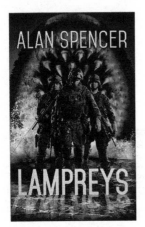

LAMPREYS
by Alan Spencer

A secret government tactical team is sent to perform a clean sweep of a private research installation. Horrible atrocities lurk within the abandoned corridors. Mutated sea creatures with insane killing abilities are waiting to suck the blood and meat from their prey.

Unemployed college professor Conrad Garfield is forced to assist and is soon separated from the team. Alone and afraid, Conrad must use his wits to battle mutated lampreys, infected scientists and go head-to-head with the biggest monstrosity of all.

Can Conrad survive, or will the deadly monsters suck the very life from his body?

DEEP DEVOTION
by M.C. Norris

Rising from the depths, a mind-bending monster unleashes a wave of terror across the American heartland. Kate Browning, a Kansas City EMT confronts her paralyzing fear of water when she traces the source of a deadly parasitic affliction to the Gulf of Mexico. Cooperating with a marine biologist, she travels to Florida in an effort to save the life of one very special patient, but the source of the epidemic happens to be the nest of a terrifying monster, one that last rose from the depths to annihilate the lost continent of Atlantis.

Leviathan, destroyer, devoted lifemate and parent, the abomination is not going to take the extermination of its brood well.

Made in the USA
Middletown, DE
29 February 2016